→ Scu
6.19.
DS 09/21

KT-450-585

This book should be returned/renewed by the latest date shown above. Overdue items incur charges which prevent self-service renewals. Please contact the library.

Wandsworth Libraries
24 hour Renewal Hotline
01159 293388
www.wandsworth.gov.uk

Wandsworth

Emma C Williams

9030 00002 3797 9

Copyright © 2012 Emma Williams

The moral right of the author has been asserted.

Apart from any fair dealing for the purposes of research or private study, or criticism or review, as permitted under the Copyright, Designs and Patents Act 1988, this publication may only be reproduced, stored or transmitted, in any form or by any means, with the prior permission in writing of the publishers, or in the case of reprographic reproduction in accordance with the terms of licences issued by the Copyright Licensing Agency. Enquiries concerning reproduction outside those terms should be sent to the publishers.

Matador
9 Priory Business Park
Kibworth Beauchamp
Leicestershire LE8 0RX, UK
Tel: (+44) 116 279 2299
Fax: (+44) 116 279 2277
Email: books@troubador.co.uk
Web: www.troubador.co.uk/matador

ISBN 978 178088 1980

British Library Cataloguing in Publication Data.
A catalogue record for this book is available from the British Library.

Cover design by Jane Brettle, Ochre Design and Artwork.
www.ochre.co.uk

Printed and bound in the UK by TJ International, Padstow, Cornwall

Matador is an imprint of Troubador Publishing Ltd

LODUGH OF
WAH

9030		
Askews & Holts	31-May-2012	
JF TEEN	£6.99	
	WWX0009336/0183	

FSC
www.fsc.org
Paper from responsible sources
FSC® C013056

For the students and staff at Woking High School.
May you all have world enough and time
to fulfil your dreams.

Chapter One

"And bend to the right?"

The Doctor's hands pushed firmly on my bony frame.

I bent my body as instructed and waited. How long was this going to go on for? I needed a wee.

"And if we could just, er, have these down a little bit further?" The Doctor pulled at the top of my pants and slid them half way down my bottom.

"And straight again," he ordered, resting both his hands on my hips.

"So, what we have here is an atypical scoliosis of the spine: classic S-shaped curve, but made unusual by this fusion of the ribs on the right hand side. This is a frequent, um, *complication* seen in this kind of syndrome."

One of the numerous medical students decided that it was his turn to make an impression.

"Might I take a closer look, Dr. Rayne?"

"Yes, yes, yes, absolutely. Everyone should be asking for a closer inspection. It's not often that you will get the chance to observe this kind of, er, *phenomenon* first-hand."

Dr. Rayne was now warming to his favourite topic. My deformity.

"Of course, when you look at the x-ray the effect is even more striking. Indeed, it's hard to believe that that this x-ray belongs to this particular child."

He patted my hips appreciatively, apparently pleased at my extraordinary ability to stand upright. Jesus. Our ancestors were standing upright two million years ago, before they developed proper human brains. So in terms of evolution, that places me somewhere just before the Neanderthals.

At least I've got opposable thumbs.

The enthusiastic medical student was now hovering behind me, hopping awkwardly from foot to foot. Dr. Rayne started pointing out notable geographical features on the landscape of my back, while the other students shuffled closer and leaned in, earnestly. As for me, I'd heard it all before and my legs were beginning to ache. How much longer? The urge to pee was rapidly becoming a far more immediate medical emergency than the long-term status of my spine. More to the point, I was also worried about the position in which Dr. Rayne had left my pants. Given that they were the only item of clothing I was allowed to keep on, I would like them to remain firmly in place; at the moment they were barely covering my pubic hair.

In total, around half of the fifteen or twenty medical students in the room made an impressive show of interest in my body during the following minutes.

They tapped and prodded with inexpert fingers, felt with hands that would one day understand what they were feeling for. A couple of them smiled at me during the process, and one of them even winked. Most avoided eye contact altogether.

You have to feel a lot of bodies before you can become an expert in them. I understand that. It just isn't much fun when you're one of the bodies being felt. And sometimes I get tired of being grown up about this sort of thing.

Ever since I can remember, I have cooperated. I have made allowances for the social inadequacy of the doctors, laughed at their bad jokes and forgiven their inability to relate to me on the grounds that they are ludicrously clever, experts in their field. I have tolerated the endless queue of anxious-looking students, surveying me with tired, hollow eyes and competing with each other to ask suitably intelligent questions. I have agreed to be photographed, scanned, x-rayed and plaster-casted. All to gather information that might, apparently, inform medical progress.

Sometimes I think they're just collecting for the sake of it, and that one day someone will clear out a filing cabinet and chuck it all away. All the pictures, casts and records of my strange and faulty packaging.

Mum was waiting outside the room as always, reading a battered-looking magazine.

"Okay?" she asked.

I shrugged. "S'pose."

"Well, let's go then. I don't see any point in talking again to Dr. Rayne, we only saw him 6 months ago."

Mum flipped her magazine carelessly back onto the table between her chair and the one that followed. Its occupant, a miserable-looking woman with a hideous toddler on her lap, looked up and scowled.

"Why we have to go through this ludicrous fiasco on such a regular basis seems a mystery to me," Mum commented, gathering up her bag and her jacket. "Still, I suppose they know what they're doing."

Dr. Rayne appeared noiselessly behind her, smiling jovially. "Indeed we do, Mrs. Jones, *indeed we do!*"

Mum pinkened slightly, but stood her ground admirably. "Well, as long as you aren't taking too many unnecessary pictures, or putting her through pointless ..."

Dr. Rayne held up his hand in an authoritative gesture of silence. "I can assure you, Mrs. Jones, that absolutely everything is entirely appropriate. We only took one x-ray this time, indeed we are trying to limit the number of x-rays overall. As I've always said, it's not good for the children to have too many x-rays. *Not good at all.*"

Mum looked irritated by his patronising tone and I could sense a debate coming.

"Mum, I *really* need a wee. Can we go now?"

Mum glanced at me and nodded.

"Right, let's get going," she agreed. "We can stop for a cup of tea and a bun in the League of Friends shop."

"That sounds just the ticket, Mrs. Jones. Marvellous little place. Give my regards to the lovely ladies behind the counter."

Christ, what a condescending cretin.

"See you in six months! Don't forget to stop by the appointments desk to book in for November."

The League of Friends shop is run by well-meaning old ladies. Not satisfied by the huge number of hours that they have to spend in hospital for the treatment of their own minor ailments, these women for some reason volunteer for extra time. How many insipid cups of tea must Mum and I have drunk from their chipped blue cups over the years? Oh, thousands. Still, it's better than going straight back to school.

"Two teas, please," Mum enunciated in crisp, ringing tones. She believes in good diction.

I hung back miserably, avoiding the tea lady's gaze. I get so tired of dealing with the way that strangers look at me. That first flicker of awkwardness when they realise that they shouldn't stare. The over-cheerful compensatory chatter with which they try to cover up their own embarrassment. That tone of voice that somehow says, "I've noticed that you're a little different, and hey, it doesn't matter! I'm such a decent person!"

Then they probably go home and tell their family what a weird looking girl they met today. "It was just as if half of her face was too small for the other half. Bits of it didn't seem to work properly, either.

Poor girl, it must be so hard. Still, she seemed bright enough."

As soon as we sat down, Mum started flipping through her diary. It appeared largely to be filled with my hospital appointments.

"You're seeing the orthodontist on Thursday and then it will be back to the Craniofacial Unit on Monday."

"But Monday's the start of Half Term!" I complained. It didn't seem fair to be stuck in a hospital for half the day without the cheering thought that I was at least missing PE.

"I know, darling, but the appointment was due and really you have missed a lot of school recently. We have to think about these things, whether you like it or not."

I drank my tea and said nothing.

"Besides, since we have to go all the way to Oxford, we might as well make it a day when we can spend the afternoon at the shops."

Ah yes, the shops. Rows and rows of clothes that aren't for me. Last week I went round the shops in Kingston with Ashley. I shouldn't have agreed to it, but occasionally I have these moments of madness, when just briefly I imagine that everything will be all right if only I could embrace the idea of acting like a normal person. Ashley meant well, but she has no idea about what I can and can't wear. She kept making ludicrous suggestions and because I kept rejecting them she told me that I was "being negative." In the end we went home.

Most of the clothes that normal people wear are a no-no for me. Catching some girls doing cruel impersonations of me in the standard school PE kit taught me that. Now I just avoid PE, as well as any kind of clothing that hints at my shape. For Dr. Rayne's eyes only. Oh, and all his students'.

Back at home Dad was mowing the lawn and the two cats were helping by getting in the way. He waved cheerfully as we arrived but kept going, a man on a mission. Mum started on the dinner and I sat in front of the television, scrolling half-heartedly through the numerous Facebook updates made by students in school during the day. "Elaine is in Maths. Sooooooo bored." "Jamie thinks Rob is gay." "Rob thinks Jamie is gay." "LMAO. Not."

God knows why I even look at these comments. Most of these "friends" don't even like me anyway, and to be honest the feeling is largely mutual. Bored with Facebook and the TV, I mooched upstairs and sat at my dressing table.

Sometimes I look in the mirror and things don't seem so bad. Maybe when the light is flattering, or a shadow falls in just the right place. I can spend hours examining myself at times like this, trying to convince myself that this better version of my face appears to the world more often than I imagine. That every time I sit face to face with Michael, *this* is what he sees.

Other times I will catch a stranger staring, or a toddler will ask its mummy what's wrong with the big girl over there, and the illusion shatters.

I am lucky to live in a big house with parents that love me. I am also lucky to be bright and talented, or so I am told. I am good at most subjects (except PE, but that doesn't count). I can play the piano. I can write well. I can act. I am good at public speaking and can put on a jolly good show of being confident as well as articulate.

But I would swap it all to be beautiful. And so would you.

Chapter Two

The first lesson the next morning was RE, and Mrs. Cameron was on particularly excitable form.

"Today we are going to debate whether abortion is acceptable or not," she announced, clasping her hands in front of her and rubbing her palms.

"Some people argue that it's a woman's right to choose, while others believe that taking a life is wrong in all circumstances."

Ashley put her hand up. "What do *you* think, Mrs. Cameron?"

"Now, what I think is not important. It's what *you* think that I'm interested in, and that's what we're going to be exploring today."

"Hmmmm. I'm quite sure she'll make her opinion apparent one way or another," I muttered.

Ashley snorted.

"Ashley, if you have something to say, you put your hand up," Mrs. Cameron said, sharply.

"But Anna just ..."

"I'm not interested."

"What about the *man's* right to choose?"

This latest comment from the back row came from Martin, who is not greatly blessed in the brains department but has a lot to say for himself anyway.

Mrs. Cameron looked exasperated. "Now let's not get into individual arguments right at the outset. First things first. We need to get into groups of four and examine the material on pages seventeen to twenty. This will give you an idea of the history behind abortion in this country."

Ashley hissed at me as thirty-one chairs scraped the floor of the classroom. "You *always* get away with it. Cambo *hates* me."

I grinned at her. "Maybe she feels like she can't pick on the weirdo kid. There have to be *some* advantages to looking like this."

"For God's sake, Anna, it's only you that's obsessed with the way you look. No-one else gives a ..."

"Ashley Wadman! If I have to warn you a third time, your name is going on the board."

Ashley rolled her eyes and made a strangled noise, somewhere between a screech and a whimper. I smiled and turned to page seventeen.

Ashley and I have been friends since primary school. Our friendship started in Year 5 when one miserable November morning both of us had sick notes to get us out of PE. We were left to tidy the lost property boxes, a task which was presumably meant to be some kind of punishment. It turned out to be the funniest thing ever. Ashley had the idea that we should perform a catwalk show for each other, using all the different clothes from the boxes. We put long football socks on our hands like evening gloves, tiny pleated skirts around our knees like fishtail hems, and shimmied up and down the hall. I don't think I have ever laughed so hard, before or since.

"The Abortion Act of 1967 revolutionised the law in England by stating that doctors could perform an abortion at any time up to twenty eight weeks," Ashley read.

"*Twenty eight weeks*?" Harry interrupted, incredulously. "Bloody hell. My sister was *born* at twenty eight weeks."

"However, the law also stated that three separate doctors had to agree to the abortion, and that it could only be performed for specific reasons: to save the life of the pregnant woman, or to prevent permanent damage to her physical or mental health."

"That's a bit weird," said Michael. "How do you prove that a pregnancy is going to affect someone's *mental* health?"

"It'd affect *my* mental health," said Harry.

"Well obviously, because in your case it would mean facing up to the truth that's been obvious to the rest of us for years – that you're actually a woman."

"I mean if a girl got pregnant, you div. And I was ... you know ... *involved*."

"She'd have to've had sex with you first, and that's never gonna happen."

I tapped the table. "For God's sake, you two. Keep going, Ashley, we've only got two more minutes to absorb this information."

"In 1990 the legal time limit was lowered from twenty eight weeks to twenty four weeks, and late abortions are only performed in very exceptional circumstances."

"Like if Harry's the father. Society must be protected," said Michael.

"Shut *up*, Michael," Ashley and I chorused, before she read on.

"This means that abortions beyond 20 weeks are very rare, and account for only around 1% of abortions performed every year in the UK."

Harry leaned back in his chair and rubbed his hand across his face. "So why do people who are against abortion always show pictures of those ones? You know, all the horrible ones. Bits of baby and stuff."

Ashley closed the text book and folded her hands. "Well, obviously because it's more powerful to show pictures of late abortions and use that to convince people that the whole thing should be stopped. It's outrageous and anti-feminist. Personally, I don't think that there should be any time limit on a woman's right to choose."

Harry stared at her. "*No time limit at all*?" he said, slowly.

"Well, all right, perhaps I don't mean *no* time limit. But I do think people spend far too much time talking about that side of things and forget what it was like for women in the old days. You know, back street abortions, hot baths and gin. Do religious people really want us to go back to that?"

"I don't think it's just religious people that are against abortion, to be fair, Ashley."

Michael spoke cautiously. You never knew when Ashley was going to kick off on feminist issues. Or religion.

"But it's *mainly* religious people. They have such strong views on things."

Harry, Michael and I all hooted with laughter.

"*What*?! What's so funny?"

I patted Ashley's arm. You've got some quite strong views on things, too, Ashley. But that's why we love ya."

"Well, I assume from the general noise level that everyone has finished reading and discussing the material," Mrs. Cameron interjected loudly. "Perhaps we can now have an informed discussion based on the facts that you have absorbed."

"And you can then steer us onto the path of righteousness," said Harry under his breath. I smiled.

"So what did people think about the general principle of 'when life begins' and how that defines the debate? Is it at the point of conception, or should we judge it as starting later on in the child's development?"

Ashley put her hand up straight away. "I think it's wrong to call a foetus "a child" until it's properly developed. To start with, it's nothing more than a ball of cells."

Emma C Williams

"And when would you argue that it is *properly developed*, Ashley?"

"When it can live outside its mother."

"Okay. Ashley has raised an interesting point, here. Some people argue that abortion should be allowed up to the point when a foetus can survive outside the womb. One problem with that view is that this time frame keeps changing. For example, there have been a couple of cases in America and Canada of premature babies surviving at 21 weeks."

Martin at the back must have woken up suddenly, and decided to grace us with his wisdom.

"I think it's out of order, Miss. A life's a life, you know? And who are we to kill it when it's got no say?"

Mrs. Cameron clasped her hands again. I sensed one of her quivering moments coming on.

"Certainly, Martin, you are expressing views held by many people. The issue of abortion is highly complex ..."

"Especially for a bear of little brain..." whispered Michael.

"... but many people *believe* that it comes down to a very simple moral principle. Does *anyone* have the right to take a *human life*?"

Jeanette at the front, who fancies herself as a bit of a geek but is actually just weird, was suddenly spurred into contributing and raised her hand.

"Miss, don't you think that sometimes, when a baby would suffer really badly, it might be the right thing to do? I mean, if it's got really awful things wrong with it and stuff."

"Ah, but Jeanette, *some* people would argue ..."

"... that "some people" being you and your church ..." murmured Ashley.

"... that all life is sacred. And that nobody has the right to decide that any one human life is worth less than another."

"Maaaaybe," said Jeanette, slowly. "But I can understand some women wanting to have an abortion. If they find out that their baby has something ... you know ... really terrible wrong with it."

This was getting interesting. I love debating and am particularly interested in moral issues. I put up my hand to make my contribution.

"*Yes*, Anna!" Mrs. Cameron re-clasped her hands in palpable delight. "I'm *so* pleased that you want to join the discussion at this particular point."

I lowered my hand slowly and stared at her. An awkward silence descended on the room.

After a few seconds, I broke it.

"What is that supposed to mean?"

Mrs. Cameron squeezed her hands and waggled her fingers.

"Well, I wondered whether you ... um ... might have some ... you know ... *poignant views* on this topic."

I continued to stare at her.

"What do you mean by "*poignant views*"?"

The silence continued. Everyone looked at me, then at Mrs. Cameron, then at me again.

"Well. Um. Only that you are perhaps someone who might ... er ... God forbid ... have been ... um ... *highlighted* in a scan as a case of ..." Mrs. Cameron trailed off helplessly.

I paused.

"There is no definitive prenatal test for Goldenhar syndrome," I said, slowly. "Some signs may be visible on a scan, but not always."

"Ah, I see! Well then."

There was another pause. Ashley stared at me, horrified.

"Are you suggesting," I said, in a careful monotone, "that had my parents known I was going to look like this then they would have had me terminated?"

Ashley put her hand on my arm. "Anna ..."

Mrs. Cameron looked terrified.

"No! No, of *course* not, Anna, that was not what I meant *at all*! I would never ... Oh goodness. Oh dear."

She wrung her hands for a few seconds.

"Look, let's move on to the next part of the discussion, shall we? The views of different religious groups?"

She looked pleadingly at me.

Suddenly, I felt weary rather than angry. I also felt sorry for Mrs. Cameron.

"Okay," I said. "Let's. As long as we can start with the Catholics."

Chapter Three

Lunchtime was awkward that day, and I was not in the mood for coping with anyone else's anxieties. I sat in silence for most of the hour, flicking through non-existent emails and text messages on my phone, listening to those around me with half an ear.

Reliably, Ashley filled the air space by regaling us with anecdotes about her pregnant cat. Judging by its size, this cat was expecting an absolutely enormous litter, and nobody knew who the father was. Chief suspect was next door's one-eyed ginger called Terrence, although an outside contender also existed in the slender form of Minky, the Siamese from across the road.

As the bell went to signal the end of the lunch hour, I gathered my things together and headed upstairs to Form Time. Michael appeared at my side and kept pace with me, hands in his pockets and head jutting slightly forward as always.

"You okay?" he asked, cautiously.

"Absolutely!" I said, trying to sound bright and casual.

"I mean about what Mrs. Cameron said. She was out of order. But I don't think she meant anything by it."

"What she *meant* by it is pretty clear."

"Okay, fair enough. But she didn't mean to make you feel bad. I think it was a misjudged attempt at saying how much ... I don't know ... how much we would all miss you. If ... if you weren't around."

There was a silence for a few seconds. Michael watched me anxiously.

Sometimes I hated it, sometimes I loved it when he looked at me closely like that. It depended on what kind of day I was having.

After a while, I met his gaze.

"I know that, Michael. That's why I'm not going to report her to the Head, which a bit of me would damn well like to. The woman's useless."

"Useless but largely harmless," said Michael. "Like Boris Johnson."

"Or Nick Clegg."

"Or *The One Show*."

I smiled, in spite of myself. "Now you're being silly."

Michael touched my arm. "Look, I'd better head on up to the second floor. If I get one more Late this week I'm in after-school detention for sure. You take care, yeah? See you tomorrow?"

I nodded.

Michael let go of my arm and I watched him as he sprinted up the next flight of stairs.

Michael first joined the school when we were in Year 8. His family had moved here from Hindhead and he managed to get a place at Manor High half way through the year. The first time I saw him he was arguing with another boy. His cheeks were flushed and his dark brown hair was falling in his eyes. From that very moment I vowed to myself that I would get close to him, and by the end of the year we were friends.

I don't want to be just friends. But friends is better than nothing.

That afternoon continued as usual, and everyone seemed to have forgotten about Mrs. Cameron's lesson. In Science we had to draw and label a diagram of the human heart, with blue arrows flowing through the right atrium and red ones through the left. I worked hard on my diagram and Mr. Brownlow commented on how good it was. Later in the lesson he made us all put our hands on our hearts to feel them beating.

In English we studied a poem by someone called Andrew Marvell. The poem was long and complex, but Mr. Randall said that it all boiled down to the poet trying to talk a woman into bed.

Some lines from the poem were beautiful and they haunted me as I walked home:

> *And yonder all before us lie*
> *Deserts of vast eternity.*

I think I know what Marvell meant by those

deserts of vast eternity. Time stretching out endlessly in front of you like the Sahara, while you ache for your life to move on.

Mum was in the middle of clearing out a cupboard when I got home, and both she and its contents were sprawled all over the kitchen floor.

"Help me with this, Anna, would you? I started this far too late in the day and I've got no idea how I'm going to get it all back in order before Dad gets home and it's time to start cooking."

I knelt on the floor next to her and started stacking tupperware boxes.

"Mum, have you heard of a poem called *To His Coy Mistress*? By Andrew Marvell?"

"You mean the one that starts *Had we but world enough and time?* The one about getting his mistress into bed?" Mum looked pleased with herself.

"That's what Mr. Randall said it was about."

Mum snapped the lid onto a plastic container and smiled at me.

"Sounds as if you don't agree with him," she said.

I thought about it for a while. "I don't know ..." I said, slowly. "Obviously that is what the poem's about. But ... but I don't think that's *all* it's about."

"Go on then," said Mum. "Enlighten me."

"It's about how it seems like things take forever, and that time just drags along and never gets moving. You know, *deserts of vast eternity.*"

Mum grunted as she climbed up off the floor.

"I remember that line," she said. But doesn't he also talk about *Time's winged chariot hurrying near*? Surely it's about filling the precious little time that we have in this world with as much worthwhile living as possible."

I sighed.

"Why do adults always go on about how short life is and how quickly time flies? It doesn't feel like that to me. Sometimes it feels like time is dragging so slowly it might as well move backwards."

Mum touched my cheek.

"It won't feel like that forever," she said, gently. "Before you know it you'll be wishing things would slow down. I promise you."

Mum's great, but I couldn't tell her about the RE lesson. I couldn't tell Dad, either. Somehow a conversation about whether they might have considered having me aborted didn't really seem a good one for the dinner table. Instead, I made both of them laugh by filling them in on Ashley's cat and its antics.

After dinner, Mum and Dad settled down to watch a boring wildlife programme and I went upstairs on the pretence of doing some homework.

Logging onto Facebook I started reading through the latest comments that people had made. Within seconds, an instant message appeared from Ashley.

"*U ok? Did u tell ur mum about 2day?*"

I wrote back.

"*No. Told her about ur cat instead!*"

"*Lol. M. said he spoke to u at the end of Lunch. He likes u a lot!!*"

My heart started beating faster. I stared at what Ashley had written for a few seconds before replying.

"*Why? Wot did he say?*"

"*Just went on how u acted like u didn't care but he could tell u were upset, etc. He's worried about you. We all are. Cambo was SO out of line.*"

My heart was still racing. Michael cares about me! Maybe I should send him a message saying thanks about today in the corridor. He was nice and I didn't say anything nice back to him. Maybe he thinks I don't care about him.

I clicked on his profile and typed.

"*U were so nice 2day. XX*"

I meant to examine the message for a while and think about whether it sounded right, but my finger got too close to the return key and within a second, there it was. On his wall. For all to see. *With two XXs!*

I stared in horror at what I had done. What was I thinking? Two XXs! Doesn't that mean something? I struggled to remember the rhyme that someone taught me in Primary School. Wasn't it "love, like, hate, adore"? So two means "like". Oh God. That's worse than "love". "Like" means "fancy."

Suddenly I noticed that there was an update. Michael had commented on my post.

"*No worries!*"

That was it. *No worries*. With an exclamation mark. And no Xs. Oh my God.

I lay down on my bed and drew my knees up. What the hell was I thinking? As if he'd actually be interested in me anyway, who did I think I was kidding? We get on, he likes me as a friend and that's it. That will always be it. Forever.

And the sooner I accept that about my life, the easier it will be.

Chapter Four

Dr. Isaac sat back in his chair and surveyed me critically. He then turned to the thick file of notes in his lap.

"How long have the top braces been on now?" he asked, flipping through my file.

"Um. About eighteen months? Something like that."

"Hmmmmm. And the bottom layer I suppose went on a little before then."

This seemed to be more in the form of a statement than a question, so I said nothing.

Dr. Isaac snapped the file shut and crossed his legs.

"The teeth still aren't entirely straight, but then I don't think they ever will be. You can't make a silk purse out of a sow's ear."

I stared levelly at him and tried not to smirk. Dr. Isaac's people skills were legendary in our family, and this was just the latest example of one of his jaw-dropping clangers. A different patient would have taken him to court for some of the things he has said to me over the years. I would enjoy telling Mum about this one later.

"The best thing we can do now is to start preparing the braces for the job that they will have to do after surgery. The sooner we get the hooks on, the sooner you'll get used to them."

"You mean the sooner I get used to the pain, the quicker it will go away?"

Dr. Isaac sniffed and clicked his pen a few times.

"You don't get rapid progress without some discomfort, I'm afraid. That's just the way it is."

If ten years' worth of orthodontic treatment can be called rapid progress, I suppose he must be right.

I lay back in the chair and Dr. Isaac got to work. While he rummaged around inside my mouth, I stared at the huge lamps on the flexible arm above his head. Two ancient cartoon stickers were fixed to the front of the glass, one of Goofy dog inexplicably doing a thumbs up, the other of a grinning Garfield. It's sobering to think how many hours of my life I have spent staring at those stickers, wishing that I were somewhere else. Do frightened younger children really find them a distraction from the fact that a grown man seems to be servicing a small car inside their mouth? I rather doubt it.

"Can't you open any wider?"

An exasperated Dr. Isaac pulled his fingers out of my mouth. His tight rubber gloves squeaked on the enamel of my teeth, and the end of one finger snapped against the wires that surrounded them.

I sighed, licked my lips and replied with exaggerated patience.

"Dr. Isaac, as I understand it, part of the reason I need surgery is because the right hand side of my jaw has not grown since infancy. Another reason, I am told, is that I have no hinge on that side. So strangely enough, no. I can't open any wider."

Dr. Isaac gave me a pained look. In ten years, he has never quite got used to the fact that this particular patient answers back.

"As wide as you can then," he said at last, and resumed his struggle.

It would probably surprise most people to know that my surgery is something that I look forward to. Hidden inside one of my drawers at home is a calendar, and every day I put a cross through the date, taking me one step closer to the long-awaited event. The calendar currently indicates that I have thirty-six days to go.

What they propose to do seems ludicrous in the extreme, indeed I am not even sure whether I believe it is actually possible. The plan is to transplant a small section of one of my ribs and somehow pin it into place where my jawbone was meant to be. They will also move some flesh around at the same time, although I am a little hazy about that side of things; it sounds like something out of a Science Fiction movie and all in all is best not considered in detail.

Most people would no doubt reel in horror at the thought of all this, but I can't wait. When you have spent every waking minute of your life dealing with people's awkward reactions to the way you look, surgery that just might put a stop to all that seems like a miracle.

It should also signal the end of all the preparation work performed by Dr. Isaac and his team, some of which has been quite frankly ridiculous. Sometimes I suspect that Dr. Isaac is writing a book about experimental braces and that I am his main subject. Over the years I have had numerous hunks of plastic and wire forced inside my tiny mouth, some of which I have point blank refused to wear for more than one day. Life's bad enough without being unable to speak without lisping or eat without gagging.

Dr. Isaac has now given up on all his grand ideas in favour of good old-fashioned train tracks, and these seem to have forced my teeth into something resembling an orderly line. That said, going by his earlier comment about pigs' ears, Dr. Isaac is clearly dissatisfied with the overall result.

Over the half an hour that I spent in his chair, Dr. Isaac attached six separate metal hooks to the braces on the top and bottom rows of my teeth. To these hooks, eventually, some other doctors would attach the wires that would hold my jaws together for six weeks once I had undergone surgery.

The last hook proved to be the biggest fiddle, and Dr. Isaac grunted with irritation as he worked. At last, he pushed himself back into his chair.

"Right," he said, peeling his gloves off and dropping them into the bin. "Time to get Mum in for a chat."

Chapter Five

I arrived back at school that afternoon to a strange reception. After signing in I had expected to return to classes immediately, but something was clearly wrong.

First of all I was asked to wait in the lobby, while one of the receptionists went over to the Head's Personal Assistant and started whispering. The assistant looked over in my direction and nodded.

What was going on?

Before I knew it, I was being ushered through and found myself waiting outside the Head's office.

"Mr. Franklin wants to interview you about some serious allegations, Anna. Wait here and he will call you in when he is ready."

This was not good.

I racked my brains, trying to think of anything that I might have done in the last few days. I had bunked a PE lesson, but that was nothing unusual. Mrs. McClain and I had a tacit understanding: I didn't go, she didn't report me, everyone was happy. She knew that I wouldn't be up to anything outrageous, just reading in the library or doing some work in a corner somewhere. So surely it couldn't be that? I cleaned my glasses with the corner of my school skirt and continued to ponder.

After about five minutes the door opened and Mr. Franklin appeared.

"Come in, Anna, come in. Take a seat here and we will discuss this business together. I hope you understand that I will need to write down what you say."

This was odd. His tone sounded nice. Nervous even. I thought I was coming in for a bollocking. Why was he smiling at me? Why was I being offered a comfy chair, in the end of the room used for friendly chats with visitors? I had expected him to be behind his desk while I stood and shifted from foot to foot in front of him. That's what Harry had said happened after he kicked that football through the Science Block window.

I sat down in the proffered seat and pushed my hands under my thighs. My heart was beating very fast. While it seemed clear now that I was not the one in trouble, I was starting to feel very frightened. Something really serious was going on. Had something happened to one of my friends? I stared anxiously at the Head while he fiddled with some papers and settled himself into the chair opposite me.

Mr. Franklin crossed his legs and surveyed me over the top of his half-moon glasses. He drummed his fingers on his knee, clearly hesitant about how he should start his opening speech. At last he began.

"Anna, a very serious allegation has been made against a member of staff. Unfortunately this allegation involves you and so I must ask you to confirm some details for me."

I stared at him. Allegation? What was he talking about? I am hardly the most obvious candidate for an inappropriate staff-student liaison, given the way I look. Isn't it normally pretty, blonde year 13 girls, who already look like they're twenty-one? No, it can't be that. So what was he on about?

"I don't understand," I said at last. "What allegation? Nobody has done anything to me. I get on fine with all my teachers."

Mr. Franklin scratched his chin with the end of his pen.

"What about Mrs. Cameron?" he asked. "Your RE teacher."

"I *know* who Mrs. Cameron is. I was in her lesson only yesterday. She's all right. She's fine. She's maybe a little biased towards the Christian perspective, but that's pretty standard for an RE teacher, isn't it?"

Mr. Franklin stared at me. He has never met me before, so isn't used to the fact that I tend to be a little straight-talking. Mum says it's the way she and Dad have raised me; she reckons that they didn't slap me down too much as a child, as they decided that I would need some fighting spirit to get me though the challenges I have to face. I say it's because most people are idiots and need things explained to them with clarity.

Mr. Franklin shifted uncomfortably in his chair.

"Anna, this is a little awkward. I am not talking about Mrs. Cameron's bias towards her own religion, although I would be interested in hearing more about that later ..."

What was this, a witch hunt? I interrupted him.

"I was only commenting on it because it's true. It doesn't make her an incompetent teacher. Mr. Brownlow's biased towards science being the greatest subject in the world ever, and he's considered to be an outstanding teacher. He *is* an outstanding teacher. He promotes Biology as being more important than any other subject, including the other sciences, *and* he's an outstanding teacher. The two aren't mutually exclusive."

"Anna, we're getting a little off track here. While I appreciate that you are an intelligent and ... um ... *highly articulate* student, it would be useful if I could explain to you what the allegation is before you make your own comments."

Right. Shut up, Anna. Give the man some space. Bless him, he's clearly struggling.

"The allegation, made by one of your fellow students this morning, is as follows. During an RE lesson, I am told, Mrs. Cameron suggested publicly that you were an example of someone who would have been better off being ... er ... terminated."

A stillness fell upon the room. I could hear the clock on the wall ticking furiously. The stools in the laboratory above Mr. Franklin's office scraped on the floor as students moved across the room to begin a science experiment.

Mr. Franklin seemed to think that his statement needed further clarification.

"According to the allegation, Mrs. Cameron stated that your parents should have decided to have an abortion."

My stomach felt tight and I started to feel hot. I glanced across to the windows, which were sealed and security locked. There should be more air in this room. How can he stand it?

"I know this must be very upsetting for you, Anna, but it is vitally important that you tell me everything so that we can deal with this. Please do not hesitate to give me all the details that you can remember."

His pen was poised and ready, hovering above the paper like a bird of prey.

I swallowed and met his gaze at last. "Mrs. Cameron did not say that," I said quietly.

"Anna, the allegation has been confirmed by several other members of the class in separate witness statements."

I felt a surge of anger. Exactly how many clandestine little chats had he been having about me behind my back?

"*Witness statements*? What is this, *CSI*? For God's sake."

Mr. Franklin looked alarmed. He spent most of his day in his office, and was not doubt unused to teenagers' emotions. As usual, it looked like I was going to have to be grown up about this.

"Look. Mrs. Cameron made a passing reference to my condition during a lesson, which she clearly realised straight away was a mistake. She just got carried away by the fact that she is strongly anti-abortion, and she struggles to keep that bias out of her lessons. She did *not* say that my parents should have had me aborted, she was actually saying exactly the opposite. Okay, I would rather she hadn't mentioned it at all, but ... give the woman a break! She made a mistake, she clearly realised that she had made a mistake, I am quite sure she won't do it again."

Mr. Franklin was scribbling on his jotter. "So what exactly *did* she say?" he asked.

"I can't remember *exactly* what she said. She got very excited because I put my hand up to join in the debate and she implied that she was particularly interested in my views."

Mr. Franklin continued to write furiously.

"Go on," he said.

"I questioned why she thought my views were so particularly relevant. "Poignant" I think was the word she used. Then she started panicking, having realised that she was digging herself into a bit of a hole."

"How exactly did she explain her interest in your *poignant views*?"

"I don't know. She started trailing off a bit, but said something like I might have been the sort of ... you know ... *foetus* that a scan would have picked up as abnormal."

"Anything else?"

"Um. Well. I told her that there isn't always evidence of Goldenhar syndrome on a scan, and then it was *me* that asked *her* whether she was implying that my parents might have considered termination as an option. She didn't actually say it."

Mr. Franklin looked triumphant. "But clearly, at the time, you thought that it was her implication."

"Maybe. But I have had time to reflect on it since. I think that she was trying, very clumsily, to make the point that all life is sacred, which is what she believes. She is a born-again Christian."

Mr. Franklin paused in his writing and looked at me hard.

"How do you know that she is a born-again Christian?"

I shook my head in disbelief. How can he be the Head of a modern comprehensive school and be so out of touch? Somebody needs to give in a lesson in modern telecommunications. He's still using a fountain pen, for God's sake.

"We Googled her. We Google all our teachers. You must know that, surely?"

Mr. Franklin put his clipboard down on the floor and rested the fountain pen on top of it. He flicked an imaginary speck of fluff from his knee and frowned.

"I was not aware that this was a common practice amongst students, no. Perhaps we should talk at greater length about this another time. For now, I think I have everything I need."

"So you're not going to have a go at Mrs. Cameron? I'm okay with what she said."

Mr. Franklin folded his arms tightly across his chest.

"Anna, this allegation is extremely serious, and becoming more so with what you have told me."

"*What?*! But I've told you she hardly said anything. Why can't that just be it? I really don't want a big fuss made out of this."

"I am afraid that the decision is not in your hands, Anna. You will have to trust us as professionals to know what is the best thing to do."

"That's ridiculous. This so-called *allegation* is all about me, so it should be me that decides what happens. I don't want Mrs. Cameron to get into trouble. She really doesn't deserve it. It was a silly mistake."

Mr. Franklin stood up from his chair and ushered me out of mine.

"Your loyalty is a credit to you, Anna, but there is no call for it. Let us handle this now, in the manner that we see fit. Time to go back to class, now."

Before I knew it I was outside his office and the door was closed. The ladies in Reception smiled at me pityingly.

Jesus. Everyone knows!

Chapter Six

I trailed miserably back to lessons to find that maths, the final lesson of the day, was almost over. Ashley was working on her own as usual. She is brilliant at maths and finds other people's incompetency with figures an irritation.

I sat down in a spare seat next to her. Mrs. Porter was at the front, marking a huge pile of books. She believes in getting on with her work while leaving us to get on with ours.

I whispered to Ashley. "Someone's reported Cambo to the Head. I've just spent three quarters of an hour in Franco's office, getting grilled about yesterday's RE lesson."

Ashley looked at me, chewing on her pen.

"Good," she said at last. "He's taking it seriously, then. I wasn't sure that he would."

She bowed her head and resumed her work.

I prodded at her. "What do you mean? Were you one of the people that he interviewed to confirm the allegation?"

Ashley sighed, laid down her pen and folded her hands in front of her. She leaned towards me earnestly.

"Anna, I *made* the allegation. And it isn't just an allegation, it's a fact. I simply told the truth. I'm not having that woman get away with this one. What she did was totally unacceptable."

I was dumbfounded. Ashley had gone to the Head. What on earth was she thinking? Was this some kind of joke?

"What possessed you? On what level did you think I would want a fuss made out of this? I just want to forget about it."

Ashley looked puzzled.

"I thought you'd be pleased that someone was standing up for you. You seemed upset about it after the lesson, and Michael said that you had mentioned the idea of going to the Head to report her. I just thought it would be much easier for you if someone else did it."

"I never said that to Michael! I mentioned that I might do so had I thought that she was being malicious. But she wasn't! She was just being an idiot, like most teachers. I don't want her to get into trouble. She might lose her job, for God's sake! How's she going to pay her mortgage?!"

Ashley waved her hand dismissively. "I think you're being just a little bit over-dramatic. She'll simply have to go through a formal disciplinary hearing."

"*What?!*"

"It's all perfectly simple. She will have to prove her competency, of course, and she'll probably have to do some further training. She won't lose her job, she'll just be monitored for a few months. Mum says it's standard procedure."

I rubbed my fingers against my temples. I could feel a headache coming on.

"You're talking about it like she deserves to go to prison. The poor woman will have to face God knows what, all because you can't keep your mouth shut. It's got nothing to *do* with you, anyway."

"It's got everything to do with me. I am a pupil in her class and I am your friend. I have every right to state my case and I did so in no uncertain terms. I'm just pleased that Franco has taken some action for once in his life."

"This is *ridiculous*," I hissed. "*You* are ridiculous. She didn't mean anything by it and I am sure she is simply mortified about that lesson. She's a nice woman."

I could feel tears pricking at the back of my eyes.

"It's not fair of you, Ashley. You shouldn't have said anything. If I don't want a complaint to be made, then there shouldn't *be* one. It's got nothing to do with anybody else."

At that moment the bell went to signal the end of school. Instantly, thirty chairs scraped across the floor, thirty bags were hauled onto thirty desks. Thirty excited students started chattering and packing away, noisily.

Ashley was particularly aggressive with her packing, slamming her bag down onto the desk and shoving her books unceremoniously into its cavernous belly.

"I simply don't understand you, Anna. You are such a demanding friend. You expect one hundred percent support from me all the time and yet you're still not satisfied. I can't get anything right and I'm sick of it. Maybe we should stay away from each other for a while if you think I'm such a liability."

"Maybe we should. And maybe you should keep your fat nose out of other people's business!"

I was shouting by now, and a couple of other students were staring. I didn't care.

"Just who the hell do you think you are? You say you're doing this to support me but it's so obvious that this is just another one of your stupid crusades. Ashley Wadman, *Human Rights Campaigner*. You don't care about me, you just like the sound of your own voice and you *love* the idea of being important. It makes me *sick*."

"*Fine! Absolutely fine!* We both know where we stand now, and as far as I'm concerned you can find yourself a new best friend. We're finished with."

Ashley slammed her way out of the room, pushing desks out of her way as she went. The last remaining students continued to stare for a while. A couple of them started to giggle.

I pushed my way past them and managed to get most of the way out of the room before the tears came.

Mum and Dad were genuinely horrified.

"I must say, darling, I think that Ashley did the right thing. Look how upset you are. This woman – Mrs. Cameron is it? – shouldn't be allowed to just get away with it.

"*Please*, Mum! You don't understand."

"Well, explain it to us, then."

I blew my nose hard.

"She made a mistake. She shouldn't have said it. I get that. But making a big deal out of it is just isn't helping."

Dad patted my hand.

"What worries me is if we just pretend this never happened then she will never learn what is and isn't appropriate. She's a professional, or at least she's supposed to be."

I sighed and wiped my nose for the hundredth time. Mum and Dad looked at each other, helplessly. After a few seconds, Mum spoke again.

"What's *really* upsetting you about all this?" she said, gently.

I took a deep breath.

"If she'd picked out anyone else in the class and made the suggestion, no-one would care. But as it's me, everyone's up in arms because ... because ... they're scared that maybe she had a point. Because ... because maybe she said what everyone else was thinking."

Mum put her head in her hands. Dad put his arm round her and at the same time squeezed my hand.

41

"Don't you *ever*, ever think that you were not wanted," he said, slowly. "You are our beautiful, talented daughter, and to us you are perfect."

At that very moment, the phone rang. Mum got up automatically.

"Leave it," Dad said.

"No, Dad, it might be Ashley."

I was already feeling guilty about the things I had said to her.

Mum picked up the phone in the study. I could hear her murmuring into the receiver.

Within seconds she had returned to the kitchen.

"Ashley's on the phone," she said. "She sounds upset."

Chapter Seven

It didn't take long to work out that both of us wanted to be friends again.

"I'm *so* sorry, Anna."

Ashley's voice trembled with emotion.

"I never meant to upset you. That's the last thing I ever want to do. I genuinely thought I was helping."

"I know, Ashley. I'm sorry too. I didn't mean any of those things. I don't think you're just a crusader. I don't know why I said it."

Ashley blew her nose.

"Harry thinks you've got a point. He reckons I should back off and leave things alone. He says I interfere too much."

I was puzzled.

"What the hell's all this got to do with Harry?"

Ashley sighed and blew her nose again. There was a long pause before she spoke.

"Look, Anna. I should have told you this before but I wasn't sure how to. Harry and I have been ... well ... sort of ... seeing each other."

I was stunned. I'd had no idea that Ashley was even interested in boys, never mind keen on one of our best friends.

"I can't believe it. Why didn't you tell me?"

"I'm not sure," Ashley said, slowly. "But I think sometimes I've wondered whether … whether you like him. In that way."

I laughed.

"Ashley, you are way off the mark. For me, it's Michael all the way."

I had said it. Out loud. For the first time.

"*Michael*?! No way! Surely not?!"

"Why? What's so weird about liking Michael? He's lovely."

"Um. Well. I don't know. He's a Christian, for starters."

I laughed again.

"Ashley, that's something you have a problem with, not me. I don't give a hoot what religion somebody is."

"Does he know?"

I paused. *Two Xs. No worries.*

"I'm not sure. Sometimes I think he must do, but I really don't know. He could have no idea whatsoever. I certainly haven't told him!"

"Why not?"

"What do you mean, *why not*?! I should have thought that was pretty obvious."

Ashley sighed.

"You know, Anna, it's never going to happen unless you let it. And that means taking some risks."

"That's easy for you to say."

"No it *isn't*. Look, everyone feels inadequate, everyone feels ugly. And all sorts of different people manage to find love. You just have to trust that it will happen."

"Now you're starting to sound like Oprah Winfrey."

"For God's sake, Anna, I'm *serious*. Stop *avoiding* this. It really is time you faced up to the fact that you're not as different from everyone else as you think you are."

There was a long silence, during which I tried to decide how honest I could bear to be.

"Listen, Ashley. I think you're imagining that my problems are the same as someone who's a bit overweight. Or who has acne. Or is convinced that no-one will fancy them because they've got no boobs. The reality for me is far more serious than that. The truth is that I am ... deformed. There's no other way of putting it."

I let that sink in for a few seconds, then continued.

"Even after the surgery this summer, things are never going to be the same for me as for everyone else. Assuming that my face does end up looking totally normal in a few weeks' time – and to be honest, I am not sure whether that will really be the case – I will still have to deal with what someone else will think when I take my clothes off in front of them."

Ashley leapt upon this.

"Well, anyone watching you take your clothes off should love you enough not to care about what they see."

"Ashley, you are so naïve. Do you *really* think that boys expect to wait until that stage to get physical? What decade are you living in?"

"I am living in the here and now thank you very much, and I stand by what I said. Why *should* you have to take your clothes off in front of someone before you know that you can trust them?"

"So you haven't taken any of your clothes off in front of Harry, yet?" I asked, casually.

"I haven't, actually. And anyway, that's beside the point."

"No it *isn't*. It's *exactly* my point. My *point* is that it will always have to be one rule for me and one rule for everyone else when that moment comes. Nobody else will have to wonder whether their potential partner will run screaming for the hills. And *that's* why it's unfair and *that's* why I don't think it's going to happen any time soon. If ever."

Ashley sighed, as if the weight of the world were on her shoulders.

"Anna, all I can say to you is that you're wrong. And at the risk of being compared again to some emotionally incontinent chat-show host, it is a fact that all sorts of people find a partner. Even Stephen bloody Hawking's got a wife!"

"Actually, he's divorced her. And she was his full-time nurse and carer. Nice comparison. Thanks."

"Anna, you are *so* infuriating! I am just trying to say that it can happen for anyone, no matter what they look like and no matter what kind of condition they're in ..."

"... you don't think it had anything to do with the fact that he's a rich guy with a terminal illness?"

Ashley let out one of her strangulated screams.

"I give up! There is just *no* point in talking to you about this."

"You've cheered me up, though. Thanks. Something about the blind, senseless optimism. Reminds me how much cleverer I am than you."

"In your dreams."

We both laughed.

"See you in the usual place tomorrow?"

"*See* ya. Wouldn't wanna *be* ya."

I hung up, smiling to myself. You just have to love Ashley.

Chapter Eight

I was seated on a tiny chair designed for five-year-olds. Surrounding me were toys and picture books. A faded "My Alphabet" poster hung at a slight angle on the wall, and sun streamed in through the sealed, double-glazed window.

"So, Anna. You know the drill. Are the headphones comfy?"

"*What*?!" I shouted, pointing to both of my ears simultaneously and tapping the side of my head. "*I can't hear you! I've got headphones on!*"

"Very amusing, Anna. If we could just get on with the test?"

Occupational Therapists. Even less of a sense of humour than orthodontists.

"So. If you would just pop one of the little sailors into the boat every time you hear a sound, that would be great."

I stared at her, then at the wooden toy boat in front of me. A line of smiling Fisher Price sailors stood to attention, ready to be slotted into the holes inside the boat.

"You *are* joking?" I queried.

"Oh, I'm sorry, Anna, I thought someone had explained this to you already. The machine we normally use for hearing tests with older children is broken. So if you don't mind, we'll have to use this method. I am sure you remember it from years ago? Just popping the sailors in whenever you hear a sound? The little ones just love it."

I don't remember loving it. I remember being bored senseless. Hey ho. Let's get on with it.

As usual, the test was extraordinarily pointless. My hearing isn't perfect but it isn't terrible. The ear on my right hand side isn't too great because the ear canal is under-developed (along with everything else on that side of my face), so the noises being pumped into that ear were notably less distinct than the ones coming into my left one.

However, given that I coped at school and managed to hear what people were saying without having to say "pardon?" the whole time, I truly did not understand the need for this process. It also annoyed me that they never gave me any results, just sent me home with a date on my appointment card for the same time next year.

Even worse was the dreaded Dr. Fuller, whose job it was to examine my ears and remove any wax that had gathered in them. I am quite sure that everyone else has wax in their ears, but for some reason wax in *my* ears in unacceptable and must be eliminated.

Dr. Fuller has a range of terrifying metal implements that he slides deep inside your ear and waggles around. The pain is simply excruciating. Anything he can't manage to get out with his metal rods he hoovers out with a miniature Dyson. This, I am told, is a highly expensive machine and apparently I am incredibly lucky to have access to it.

Dr. Fuller is the only medical professional that reduces me to tears on most visits. Trust me: if anyone suggests to you that your ears need cleaning out, run like hell.

At school I was horrified to discover that today Mrs. Cameron was to be forced to apologise to me. My parents had already received a letter from her in which she expressed her "sincere regret for the distress that her comments may have caused." The whole thing was clearly written by Mr. Franklin and my parents were singularly unimpressed with its obsequious tone.

The letter promised that Mrs. Cameron would be apologising to me in person prior to the next RE lesson. It also stated that this momentous event would take place in Mr. Franklin's office. How simply horrendous. It appeared that no-one cared how I felt about the whole thing, just so long as the "right thing" was seen to be done.

On arrival I was ushered in by Mr. Franklin's Personal Assistant with the usual air of officialdom. She simply loves this kind of thing. I guess it makes her feel important, like she's working for a lawyer or something.

Mrs. Cameron was already waiting inside the office, sitting on a chair in front of the Head's desk. No cosy-corner chat this time, then.

"If you would like to take the seat next to Mrs. Cameron, Anna?"

I did as instructed, and waited for Mr. Franklin to settle himself behind his desk. I couldn't look at Mrs. Cameron.

Mr. Franklin pushed some papers to one side and leaned his elbows on the desk. Interlacing his fingers, he surveyed the pair of us with a tangible air of ceremony. What an *arse*.

"Right, Anna. As you are aware, we are here so that Mrs. Cameron can apologise to you in person for the comments that she made on June 21st during an RE lesson."

"Yes."

"You should already have received a written apology, but Mrs. Cameron and I feel that it is important to ... um ... *clear the air*. Just to ensure that we can all move on from this."

I was quite sure that Mrs. Cameron was about as happy with this buttock-clenching scenario as I was, but no doubt she had been given no choice in the matter either.

"So, turning to you, Mrs. Cameron. I think now is the appropriate time to set the record straight."

Mr. Franklin waited in expectant silence. I looked at the floor.

"Anna, I don't know what to say."

Mrs. Cameron sniffed and wiped her nose with a tissue. Horrified, I realised that she was crying.

"I would never deliberately do anything to upset a student, and I feel totally wretched about what I have done. I wish I could undo it, but I can't. What I said was totally wrong and you must have been ... devastated."

This last word came out as a whimper, and for reasons I cannot explain I felt tears pricking at the back of my eyes. I blinked furiously and continued to stare at the floor. A small spider was dangling on an invisible thread from Mr. Franklin's desk. I wondered how long it had been there.

Mrs. Cameron blew her nose and took a deep, shuddering breath in an attempt to compose herself.

"Please accept my sincerest apologies, Anna. I hope that you can forgive me?"

Miserably, I kept my stinging eyes focused on the floor and said nothing. I was desperate not to cry in front of Mr. Franklin. He must be loving this.

"Anna? Do you accept Mrs. Cameron's apology?"

I nodded, grasping the opportunity to communicate without the use of eye contact or my voice.

"Fine. Enough, then. I think that Mrs. Cameron has apologised sufficiently so that we can all move on from this. No more discussion."

I felt a surge of anger. It was only he that had insisted on a discussion in the first place! Who the hell does he think he is, some kind of UN Ambassador? The whole thing was ludicrous.

Mrs. Cameron seemed to have recovered herself a little and she straightened up in her seat.

"If you will permit me, Mr. Franklin, I feel strongly that it is entirely appropriate for Anna to witness my formal resignation."

Mrs. Cameron passed a slim, white envelope across the desk.

"I feel that I can no longer continue to teach in this school. My Union assures me that you are unlikely to insist I work through to the end of my contract, as would normally be expected."

Union? Contract? This was getting silly. It's about time someone acted like a grown-up and what do you know, it would have to be me again.

"Sir, please don't accept it. This is all completely unnecessary."

But Mr. Franklin could barely contain his obvious delight.

"Anna, if Mrs. Cameron feels that this is the best course of action for her, I am not inclined to argue."

Within seconds the white envelope was settled in Mr. Franklin's in-tray, and I was ushered out of my seat again.

There are not many pupils that can claim the dubious honour of being the cause of a teacher's resignation. Somehow, inexplicably, I was now one of them. What on earth would everyone think?

Chapter Nine

I had hardly seen Michael since the *no worries* comment on Facebook. He had missed several lessons playing cricket for the school team, and it was not until RE the next day that we found ourselves in a lesson together.

By the time we were all filing in that morning, news of Mrs. Cameron's demise had spread right across the school. Fortunately, my involvement had largely been forgotten in favour of lurid rumours about her incompetency. Most people thought that she had been sacked by Mr. Franklin for failing to stick to the correct syllabus in her exam classes; I was not about to enlighten them as to the truth.

Stood at the front of our class that morning was a tiny, bird-like creature. She was dressed in clothing that was slim-fitting but that covered every part of her, including a tightly-bound headscarf that covered her hair and surrounded her face. She introduced herself as Miss Khan.

"I believe that you have recently covered the abortion debate. Today we will move on to euthanasia. Martin, have you heard of euthanasia?"

She knew his name already. How?

Martin instinctively sat up straighter in his chair.

"Um. Yeah. I've heard of it."

"What does it mean?"

"Um. I don't know."

Miss Khan's eyes scanned the room and she selected another victim.

"David?"

She knew his name as well! Amazing.

David fared slightly better.

"Isn't it that thing where people go to Switzerland?"

Miss Khan pointed her finger in David's direction and waggled it.

"David is referring to *Dignitas*, Europe's first purpose built centre for assisted dying. But that is not quite what we're talking about. What is *euthanasia*?"

This was getting painful. I raised my hand.

"Yes, Anna?"

Teachers always know my name, so no surprises there.

"Euthanasia literally means *good death* or *dying well*. It is the term applied to the ending of someone's life in order to end their suffering."

"Well done, Anna, particularly for showing your understanding of the term's origin. Let's focus on that to start with. *A good death*. What do people think about that phrase?"

The class sat in stunned silence. This wasn't the usual deal. We weren't supposed to think in RE, it was meant to be easy.

Miss Khan clarified her question, spreading her arms wide as she did so.

"Can death ever be good?"

Jeanette put her hand up hesitantly.

"Yes, Jeanette?"

Harry prodded me in the back. "This is getting spooky," he whispered. "What did she do, stay up all night learning the register of the entire school?"

Miss Khan raised her hand authoritatively.

"If Harry would stop distracting other people, we can hear Jeanette's answer. Go on, Jeanette."

"Um. I think death can be good when it relieves suffering. We had our dog put down because it was in pain."

"Okay. This is what we are going to focus on today, and I want you to try to set aside any preconceptions that you may already have. I am going to give you a series of statements about euthanasia and about assisted suicide. Some of them are facts and some of them are opinions."

"A sorting exercise!" hissed Ashley. "Yippee! Now we're back on familiar territory."

"Ashley, perhaps you would like to hand out the cards, since you seem so confident that you can do the task."

Ashley rolled her eyes at me as she left her seat, but did as she was told.

We settled to the task, working in our usual group of four. Up to this point I had avoided Michael's gaze. Sitting opposite him and having to take part in a discussion, some eye contact was unavoidable. When my eyes finally met his, he was smiling as usual.

"Listen to this one," he said, holding up a card:

"Either life is always and in all circumstances sacred, or intrinsically of no account; it is inconceivable that it should be in some cases the one, and in some the other."

"Who said that?" Ashley asked.

"Some bloke called ... er ... Malcolm Muggeridge.

Ashley snorted.

"So what do we think of that as an opinion?" said Michael. "Are we going to say that we disagree with it? What do you think, Anna?"

"Um. Personally I disagree with it."

Harry took the card and placed it down on the desk.

"Me too," he said. "I think we should disagree on principle with anything said by someone whose name makes them sound like a character in *Harry Potter*."

"That is a simply ridiculous reason and you know it," said Ashley, sharply.

"Maybe, but we've got three minutes to do this!"

"Good point," said Michael. "So, anyone with a name even vaguely resembling someone or something involved with witches or wizardry gets banished to the 'no' column."

He winked at me, fanning through the pile of cards in front of him like a professional gambler.

"Next card," he said, and produced it with a flourish.

Having examined the card, Michael flopped forward on to the desk, shoulders shaking.

"Okay, who said this next one?" I said, smiling in spite of myself.

"Someone ... called ... Ecclesiastes!" yelped Michael, in between wild snorts of laughter. "Now if he's not a wizard, I don't know who is!"

"It's a book of the Bible, you idiot! Old Testament!" I pulled the card from under his arms. "You should know that, out of all of us!"

"You are correct, Anna," said Miss Khan, who had magically appeared at our table. "*No man has power over the wind to contain it; so no one has power over the day of his death.* I have always thought it to be one of the most beautiful lines in the Old Testament."

Despite my residual guilt about Mrs. Cameron, I couldn't deny that it was the best RE lesson I had ever experienced, and you could tell from the atmosphere that I was not the only one who felt like this. As we poured out of the school and into the sunshine, everybody was talking about the lesson and about Miss Khan. Everybody, that is, except Michael, who had more important things on his mind.

"Listen, guys! It's my brother's 18th birthday this weekend and Mum and Dad have finally agreed that he is old enough to be in charge of a party at home without them hovering around, re-arranging the Twiglets. My brother says I can ask whoever I want! I'm going to ask pretty much everyone I know, including the cricket team. It should be amazing!"

"What's so amazing about the cricket team?" asked Harry. He has a bit of an issue with the fact that he isn't too great at contact sports.

Ashley and I looked at each other. She was grinning.

"Count us in!" Ashley whooped and starting spinning around like a whirling dervish.

Harry grabbed her round the waist and swung her around with him. They both fell onto the grass, laughing raucously.

It was the first time that I had seen them act like a couple in front of me, and I felt a pang of jealousy.

Please, God. Let that be me one day.

Chapter Ten

That Saturday afternoon, Ashley and I spent several hours at my house getting ready for the party. From the very outset, Ashley made it clear that I was having a makeover.

"I've been thinking, Anna. If we do your hair in a sweep to one side, it will really work."

Ashley demonstrated by swishing my hair over to the right in a makeshift ponytail. Under her expert manipulation, my wavy hair fell obediently into soft folds across the right hand side of my face.

"See what I mean?"

I did see, and I was excited. Why on earth hadn't I let Ashley loose on my hair before? Her own hair always looks amazing and she manages to tie it in a hundred different ways. This was going to be brilliant.

While Ashley spent half an hour trying on the various different combinations of clothes that she had brought as possible outfits for the evening, I ran myself a deep and sweet-smelling bath. Settling into its comforting warmth, I soaped up my legs and started shaving.

I have always liked my legs. They are one of the significant parts of me that are not only normal but are actually rather good. While others have been cursed with short, stumpy calves or wobbly thighs, my legs are slim and shapely. I shaved carefully, avoiding any possibility of nicks or cuts, and thought about the evening to come.

Michael had been really enthusiastic about this party and I wondered why. Certainly he was happy that his new mates from the cricket team would be there, but he seemed equally delighted that we were coming too. Although part of me knew it was crazy, I couldn't help getting excited and hopeful about tonight.

Surely Michael must know by now that Ashley and Harry had paired up? Wouldn't he be avoiding us hanging out as a foursome if the idea of being paired up with me filled him with horror? Maybe, maybe.

After my bath and when I had smothered my legs in moisturiser, Ashley set to work on my hair and makeup. In less than an hour, she had worked a miracle.

Using hair grips and ties, she secured my long hair in a series of folds sweeping over to the right. Loose tendrils fell across my right cheek, softening the angular appearance of my crooked chin and screening the irregularity of my jawbone. With minimalist makeup she shaded and highlighted to emphasise my normal features, and used mascara to draw attention to my eyes. Even behind my glasses the lashes looked luscious and long. I was speechless.

Together we selected the outfit that suited me most from my collection of clothes: a loose-fitting, high-waisted floaty top slung over tight shorts that finished just above the knee, to show off my legs.

Ashley stood back, hands on hips.

"There you go," she said, with an air of pride and satisfaction. "You look amazing."

For once, I agreed. I felt so happy.

"Ashley, I don't know what to say. You are a miracle-worker. I can't believe how good I look!"

Ashley sat down on my bed and indicated that I should do the same. I sat next to her and she put her hand on my shoulder.

"Listen, Anna. The main reason I have done this is to prove to you that you *are* the same as everyone else. You'll have good days and bad days; days when you look and feel great, days when you look and feel horrendous."

I tried to think of a day when Ashley had looked horrendous, but couldn't.

"The important thing is to make the best of what you've got. You have amazing legs, lovely hair, good skin and you're slim. There's plenty of girls would kill for just one of those assets."

True, all true.

"That said, the other thing you must remember is that none of this matters anyway. It's not about what you look like, it's about finding someone that values you for who you are. Someone that will listen to you and understand when you've had a crap day. If you think that someone is Michael, then ... then you should go for it."

I smiled at her.

"Even if he is a Christian? And I think his parents vote Tory."

Ashley sighed.

"Even if he's a Christian and even if he's going to be the next Tory Prime Minister. I don't care. Whatever makes you happy."

I hugged her.

"I don't know what I would do without you, Ashley. You are such a fantastic friend. I'm sorry I'm such a pain in the arse a lot of the time."

Ashley squeezed me hard.

"I don't know what you're talking about," she said. "You are nothing but reasonable, all of the time."

We both laughed.

"So. Are we ready to go to this party?"

"Absolutely."

Chapter Eleven

My Dad drove us to the party. Ashley and I sat in the back of the car in a state of high excitement.

"When's Harry arriving?" I asked.

"He's probably there already. Michael asked him to go over early so that they could have some say in his brother's choice of music for the evening."

"Fair enough. You know what Simon's like, it'll be nothing but Kanye West if he's got anything to do with it."

Harry was indeed already there when we arrived. He and Michael were both dressed in low-slung jeans and T-shirts. Michael was debating with his brother about where they should put the punch bowl.

Ashley and I sat down on a bench in the garden and tried not to look too excited. Simon grunted to us and raised his can of beer as he walked past, which we agreed between ourselves was an older boy's version of a thoroughly magnanimous welcome.

Michael's Mum and Dad were still around, but were preparing to spend the evening at a local restaurant. Michael's Dad performed some last-minute checks on the sound system inside the conservatory. He then gave his two sons a final pep-talk about responsibility. Ashley and I distinctly heard the word *shenanigan* and the phrase *general monkey business* being used during his little speech. There was also a good deal of finger-pointing and nose-tapping. We held each other up as we shook with silent laughter at what was quite possibly the funniest thing we had ever seen and heard.

The departure of Michael's parents seemed magically to trigger a flurry of guests. Numerous older boys arrived in a steady stream, each as monosyllabic as the last. Most of them hung around the table where the beers were stacked. Some of them were smoking, although they didn't look like they were enjoying it very much.

By the time all of Michael's guests had arrived, the music was on and the pile of beers was diminishing rapidly. Simon's mates started playing a game that involved firing stones at empty beer cans. There was a lot of whooping and roaring, although it was hard to see exactly what was so exciting about it. Maybe it was better if you had actually drunk the beer inside the cans.

Simon had also asked some older girls to the party. They surveyed us coolly from a distance and let the older boys light cigarettes for them. One of the girls wore tight hot pants and a bikini top. The boys couldn't take their eyes off her. Ashley said that she looked like a skank, but I thought she looked stunning.

Ashley and I spent the first half of the evening mouthing the words *monkey business* and *shenanigan* at each other and giggling helplessly. I overheard one of Simon's mates commenting that we were pathetic. I didn't care. We were having the time of our lives.

Michael spent the first hour or so joking with Harry and with his friends from the cricket team. I didn't know many of them, but they seemed okay. It would have been nice if Michael had introduced us properly, but maybe that would happen later.

After the first hour, Harry came over to where Ashley and I were sitting. He sat next to Ashley and put his arm round her shoulders.

"I'm bored with that lot," he said, yawning. "All they talk about is cricket."

"You're just annoyed because you're crap at cricket," said Ashley, fondly.

"Maybe. But I stand by the fact that they're boring. One of them's called *Jeremy*."

Ashley and I hooted with laughter.

"Case closed!" I said. "He *must* be boring if he's called *Jeremy*."

"Well quite."

We sat in silence for a while. It was hard to admit, but the whole evening was starting to feel like it might just become a little bit dull.

"Why don't we play a game?" said Harry at last. "Names for posh boys, one for each letter of the alphabet. We start with A and then go round in a circle. No repetition, deviation or hesitation. I'll start."

"Right. Go on then."

"Um. Right."

"You said no hesitation!" said Ashley.

"Well, all right, you start then."

"No, no! Your game, you start."

"Right. Ambrose."

"Brett."

"Clifford."

"Douglas."

"Erm ... Ebenezer."

Harry howled at Ashley's last suggestion. "Hesitation! And anyway ... *Ebenezer*?!"

"Apparently it's very popular in some circles."

"I don't believe you."

"What's all the hooting about?"

Michael had appeared. He settled himself down on the bench next to me and leaned forward, grinning.

Harry, Ashley and I looked at each other.

"We were just playing a word game," said Harry. "Names of ... of animals."

"Sounds like you guys are getting bored. Why don't I introduce you to some of the others?"

At last!

"Guys!" Michael shouted. "Why don't you come over here and meet my RE pals?"

RE pals? How odd.

Three members of the school cricket team sauntered over and sat down. Michael performed some perfunctory introductions and everyone nodded. We all then forgot each other's names immediately, or at least I did.

"So," said Michael, leaning back and stretching. "This is Anna. The one I've just been telling you about. She's amazing."

The boys nodded in knowing recognition. My heart started beating more quickly. I was acutely aware that Michael's right arm was resting on the back of the bench behind me. I could feel its warmth on the back of my neck.

"Anna's going to be famous one day, there's no doubt about that. I think she'll either be a writer or a lawyer."

"My Dad's a lawyer," said one of the cricketers. "He says it's a shit job with long hours."

"Well, a writer then. Either way, she's going to be a real success. Aren't you, Anna?"

I didn't really know how to reply to this. For some reason, Michael seemed to be talking about me like a proud parent. It was all very strange. Fortunately, while I pondered how I should respond, the attention of the cricketers surrounding us was caught by another member of the team.

"Lads! I've found a tennis ball!"

Our three companions leapt up like excited dogs and lolloped over to where a makeshift cricket game was starting.

"So much for conversation!" said Ashley, sarcastically. But all I felt was relief.

Then something wonderful happened.

Michael slid his arm down from the back of the bench and around my shoulders. His fingers curled round the top of my arm and squeezed it. I held my breath.

"I really hope we never lose touch, Anna," he said. "My parents are talking about moving back to Hindhead this summer. Dad's job is finished, and they don't really like it here."

My heart was pounding in my chest.

"Hindhead's not that far away," said Ashley. "You can always stay in touch."

"Yeah," said Harry. "You can't split up the Fab Four."

Michael squeezed my arm again. I was lost for words.

"You're right," he said. "There's always Facebook."

There was a pause during which none of us said anything. At last, Michael broke the silence.

"Anyway. I'd better go and refill that punch bowl."

And before I knew it, he had given me a final squeeze and was walking away.

"*Oh my God!*" Ashley hissed. "Harry and I had better give you some space!"

"Eh?" said Harry. "What are you on about?"

"Michael and Anna, you Dumbo. Surely you must have noticed?!"

"I thought he was just being friendly."

"Honestly, boys know nothing. Anna, we'll go and take over from Michael with the punch bowl.

Hopefully he'll take the initiative and come straight back over. *Good luck!* And don't play it so *cool* this time – he's made a move, *it's now or never!*"

With that, she and Harry were gone as well, leaving me on the bench to ponder what she had said. Somehow I just knew that she was right. Michael and I both needed to know where we stood and it was time I stopped running away from this. He had reached out to me and I had said and done nothing. If I wasn't careful, I would end up rejecting what I wanted most!

After what seemed like an eternity Michael came back alone, and this time I was ready.

I smiled at him as he sat down and he smiled back. His eyes looked a little apprehensive.

"Hey you," he said, gently.

Hesitantly, I rested my hand on his knee and squeezed it. He let it stay there.

Thank you, God.

We sat there for a few seconds and listened to the birds mingled with the shouts of the cricketers and the roar of Simon's mates. It was quite possibly the most perfect moment of my life.

"Listen, Anna," said Michael at last. "I don't quite know how to put this, but ..."

He swallowed.

"... but something Ashley has just said got me worried."

He patted my hand affectionately, then held on to it.

"You know I think you're simply amazing, don't you? I mean really, really amazing. You're like ... my role model. I've never known anyone quite like you."

He paused and scratched the back of his neck with his other hand.

"The thing is ... I ... God, this is hard. The thing is ... I think that I may have given you the wrong impression just now. And maybe at other times. I don't know. The *truth* is ... I just ... I just don't see you ... *in that way*. You know?"

He squeezed my hand and looked at me, anxiously. The cricketers continued to yell and Simon and his mates continued to roar. The birds were still singing in the trees.

"Anna? I hope it's okay? I meant everything I said about you being amazing and about us staying in touch. I bore my mates silly with how clever you are. My Mum and Dad, too."

"I understand," I said at last, and at that point the tears began to trickle slowly down my cheeks.

"I understand perfectly. Everything about me is terrific. Except the packaging."

"Oh, Anna. That's not how it is."

"Yes it is!" I cried, snatching my hand away. "I wish everyone would stop God damn *pretending*. That's *exactly* how it is!"

Tears were pouring down my cheeks now, and I didn't care.

"I am sitting here with one of my best friends telling me that *everything* about me is wonderful but that they *still* can't see me in that *way*. If that doesn't tell me everything I need to know, then I'm a fool. And so are you. A fool or a liar."

I stood up from the bench and ran towards the house, wiping furiously at my face with my sleeve. I could hear Michael shouting behind me.

"Anna! Anna! Come back! Don't run away like this!"

I ignored him and didn't stop until I found the bathroom. I locked the door, crawled into a corner beside the basin, put my head onto my knees and howled.

Chapter Twelve

The NHS mean what they say when they use the phrase *Waiting Room*. Five days after the horrors of Michael's party, Mum and I had been sat for almost two hours at Moorfield's Eye Hospital, Marylebone.

Mum is used to waiting, and so am I. We can wait for hours if necessary, flipping through dog-eared copies of *Woman's Weekly* and passing judgement on the colour schemes of our dismal surroundings.

When it comes to selecting the plastic chairs used for most NHS waiting rooms, bile green seems to be the preferred choice of colour. Mum has mused in the past that it seems to be designed to resonate with how sick the patients might be feeling. If the preferred shade of bile is not available then brilliant orange is always a fine choice, and this was the option that Moorfields had plumped for.

It was a particularly hot day and it didn't take long for my legs to find themselves glued to the plastic seat. Every minute or so I would peel one of them off and move it slightly so that it could have a few seconds of respite before adhering itself to the seat again.

As the minutes continued to tick by with no apparent sign of progress and no apologies volunteered by the staff, Mum decided that she should go and investigate what the nearest vending machines had to offer.

"If the tea looks closer to brown than grey shall I bring you one?"

"Ah, bring me one whatever the colour. I like to live life on the edge."

With Mum gone, I returned to my year-old edition of *Woman's Weekly*. My attention had been caught by the story of Donna (*names have been changed*), who was 28 stone and pregnant with her fifth child, father unknown. Jesus. If ever I wanted proof that *any* woman can find some action if she wants it, here it was. On the other hand, when I look at the rogue's gallery of specimens that she's had to settle for, I think I'd rather take the celibacy option.

"Have you read the story about the sex-crazed granny yet?"

A male voice cut across my thoughts and I started up from my reading.

Sat opposite me was a skinny boy of about my age, although he could have been a little younger. He had extremely thick glasses that seemed rather too large for him and straight black hair combed to one side.

He wore a black T-shirt bearing the image of a devil holding an electric guitar. Above this was the logo *Monsters of Rock*. The T-shirt was tucked into faded black jeans that were slightly too short for him, revealing grey school socks slipped into Velcro trainers.

"Those magazines are hilarious," he said, indicating the *Woman's Weekly* in my hands. "I'm thinking of writing a "true life story" for one of them. They don't care whether it's true or not. And they pay you £200!"

"If they didn't care whether the stories were true surely they would just make them up in the office and save themselves the money?"

"Hmmm. Maybe you have a point. In that case, perhaps I'd better claim that I am bed-bound and suffer from social phobia, so can only contact them by email. Then all I would need is a picture of a suitably overweight woman in a bed looking miserable."

I considered this.

"Yep. That might work. You could easily set up a fake email address under a woman's name."

"Absolutely."

"What would you call yourself?"

"Good question. How about ... Tracy. Or Sheryl. Something suitably chavvy."

He paused for a moment.

"Shit. I've just thought. You're name's not Tracy or Sheryl is it?"

I laughed.

"No, no, you're quite safe. My name's Anna."

He gave a mock bow.

"Nice to meet you, Anna. I'm Tim."

I nodded.

"So. At the risk of sounding cheesy ... come here often?"

I snorted.

"Unfortunately yes. How about you?"

"All the time. Apparently I have a particularly unusual astigmatism that needs regular monitoring."

He said this with a sense of pride that irritated me. Only someone who didn't have to spend half their life in hospital waiting rooms would be chuffed about it. I changed the subject.

"So who are the *Monsters of Rock*?" I asked, indicating the image on the front of his T-shirt.

"It was a rock festival in 1991. *AC-DC* and *Metallica* were the headline bands. Heard of them?"

I hadn't.

Tim stood up and turned around to reveal the back of the T-shirt, which was even worse than the front. Sure enough, the date of August 17th 1991 was emblazoned across the bottom half.

"But you wouldn't have even been *born* in 1991," I said. "Why are you wearing it?"

Tim strode across the waiting room and sat down next to me.

"My brother was there and he got me interested in heavy metal music. I'm really into it now. *Guns n Roses* especially."

I hadn't heard of *Guns n Roses* either, but I was pretty sure I wouldn't like them.

Tim pointed to the top half of his right arm.

"One day I'm going to get a tattoo dedicated to

them. Right here."

I nodded but couldn't think of anything to say.

"I'll have to wait until my eighteenth birthday. You have to be eighteen to get a tattoo."

I tried to imagine Tim's scrawny arm sporting a tattoo, but it was unthinkable.

"I think you have to be big and muscular to carry off a tattoo," I said at last.

"What are you suggesting? That I'm a wimp?"

Tim flexed his puny biceps with exaggerated pride.

"I don't know what you're talking about, Anna. "Just look at my bulging physique. Sometimes, I just don't know how the ladies resist."

At that moment a nurse in white trousers and a navy tabard appeared in the waiting room, holding a clipboard.

"Tim Stademan?"

"Damn, that's me. Listen, Anna, you're great and I'd like to stay in touch."

I couldn't believe it. Was this guy serious?

"Are you on Facebook?"

"Er ... yes."

"Look me up. *Tim Stademan*. And I'll look you up. Anna ...?"

"Er ... Jones."

"Right. You'd better make sure you look me up, then! I'll never find you amongst all the other Anna Joneses. *Stademan. Tim Stademan*. You won't forget?"

"How could I?"

"Brilliant. Speak later, then."

And with that he lolloped off to follow the nurse, almost colliding with Mum as she returned with the teas.

Mum sat down next to me, holding two polystyrene cups gingerly.

"I know that boy," she said, handing one of them to me. "I've spoken to his Mum a couple of times in the waiting room. Is he here on his own today?"

"Looks like it."

"Perhaps his Mum is having a bad day. She has Multiple Sclerosis."

I stared at her.

"How the hell do you know that?"

"As I said, I have spoken to her a couple of times. She's in a wheelchair and she told me the reason why. She says the pain comes in waves and that some days she finds it difficult to leave the house."

Mum sipped her tea, wincing visibly at the taste.

"Apparently Tim knows how to make his own way to the hospital by train when he needs to. He's very independent for his age. I guess he's had to be."

"What about his Dad? Couldn't he come with Tim when his Mum's ill?"

"Tim's father is dead. He died four years ago of a heart attack."

I sat and absorbed this information for a while, feeling guilty that I hadn't been a bit nicer.

"Tim and I got talking," I said at last. "He wants me to look him up on Facebook."

"Well that's nice! You should do that. Tim's mum says that he is highly intelligent. Apparently he is at the very top of the Gifted and Talented register at his school, whatever that means."

"He's a bit ..."

"A bit *what*?"

"Er ... sad."

Mum tutted with exasperation.

"Honestly, Anna, I would have expected better from you."

She picked up her magazine and started turning the pages.

Chapter Thirteen

I have virtually no sight in my right eye and for reasons that have never yet been explained to me, Dr. Wells at Moorfield's Eye Hospital has to confirm this once a year.

I suggested to him once that I could save him a lot of time and the NHS a lot of money by emailing confirmation of my lack of sight on a yearly basis. He smiled and shook his head, as did the two nursing assistants behind him.

So this year, like every year before it, I demonstrated once again for him that my right eye could not see the big letter H at the top of the board; indeed, it could not see the board at all. I let him shine his little torch into it and answered his pointless questions as best I could. No, I did not get headaches. Yes, it did affect my hand-to-eye coordination. No, this was not a problem as I had no plans to become a professional tennis player.

Mum decided that after our extended encounter with *Woman's Weekly* and by the time Dr. Wells had proved once again to his satisfaction that my right eye was a dismal failure, it was too late to battle through the traffic and get me back to school.

This was a huge relief for me, as every moment spent in school since last Saturday was time spent trying to avoid Michael. Fortunately I had Ashley's support in this, so our encounters had been minimal: Ashley had made Harry promise to keep Michael out of my way and he had done as he was asked. My closest contact with Michael had therefore involved passing him in the corridor. He had ignored me and I had ignored him. And so it was to be.

Mum was right about the traffic. By the time we were home we were both exhausted and school had finished an hour previously. Mum kicked off her shoes and opened a bottle of wine while she started on the dinner. She usually waits for Dad, but some days she reckons she deserves to start early.

I hadn't been intending to take Tim up on his suggestion that we hook up on Facebook, but Mum's insights into his life had made me feel guilty. If his mum was ill and his Dad was dead, it seemed a bit harsh to ignore his quest for friendship. I went upstairs and logged on to my computer.

He wasn't difficult to find. There were only three Tim Stademans on Facebook and his smiling, beaky face was clearly pictured next to one of them. I clicked "Add as friend" and barely had time to start checking my messages before my request was accepted. Tim was online.

Hey, Anna. Great to hear from you! How was your appointment?

I sighed. Clearly Tim was expecting to have a conversation. I considered logging off but I knew that this was just mean, so I replied in a manner that I hoped was polite but minimalist.

Not bad. Yours?

Likewise. Not sure why they bother, there never seems to be any change from one year to the next.

Tim's online style was unusual. No abbreviations, no text speak, no spelling mistakes. Part of me was impressed; part of me felt inexplicably irritated. He continued.

So what's happening for you this weekend? Up to anything exciting?

This was turning into a lengthy conversation, and I was hoping to scupper it as quickly as possible.

Not really.

That should do it. Surely he would eventually get the hint.

Brilliant. Want to meet up in London?

I stared at the screen in horror. One minute I was reluctantly entering into a conversation I did not really wish to have, the next minute I was painting myself into the corner of meeting up. Why hadn't I said that I was busy?

Tim obviously sensed the delay and decided to offer some words of encouragement.

It's okay. I know my way around London. You'd be in safe hands.

Yeuch. *Safe hands.* It doesn't even bear thinking about. Was this a *date*? I considered my reply carefully, and decided to blame my reluctance on my parents.

I don't think Mum and Dad would let me go into London on my own.

Tim's reply was swift and confident.

Sure they will. You wouldn't be on our own, and your Mum knows my mum. Say it's with me and I'm sure they'll say yes. Tell them it's educational. We could go to the British Museum. Or the National Gallery. Whatever you want.

I didn't *want* to go anywhere with Tim, but somehow it seemed inevitable. I couldn't think of a single reason to say "no", other than the fact that I found him physically repellent, which was not something that I was cruel enough to share with him.

I moved away from my computer and lay on the bed, knees drawn up under my chin.

When you look the way I do, you spend much of your time imagining how great it would be if the world were different. If people didn't judge each other based on appearances, or if we were all blind to the very difference between beauty and the grotesque.

But the truth about how I feel is far less noble than that. The truth is, I wouldn't prefer a different world. I want *this* world, but I would like to be one of the lucky people: the people who get stared at for the right reasons.

And I don't want someone who will love me as I am; I want to be someone that is easy to love.

And most of all, I don't want to be seen with

someone like Tim and know that the world is thinking *… this is the best that I can do.*

I sat up on the bed and sighed. There was no getting away from the fact that I was as shallow as everyone else. How awful is that? All the experiences that I have been through, you'd think they would make me a better person. Apparently not. How depressing.

I dashed back to the computer and typed a reply before I could change my mind.

Okay. I'll ask them.

Chapter Fourteen

Unsurprisingly, Mum and Dad were a little dubious about my recent foray into what they termed "internet dating."

"It's not a *date*, Mum! And it's certainly not an "*internet date*" as you call it. I met Tim at the hospital. It just so happens that he has used Facebook as a method of staying in touch. That's pretty normal these days, you know. There's nothing creepy about it."

Dad cleared his throat.

"So who is this Tim chap, and what are his intentions?"

"Dad, for God's sake, it's not the 1950s. He's not a *chap* and he doesn't have any "intentions" other than to go to the British Museum. To be perfectly honest I don't particularly want to go, but he's been very friendly and I feel mean refusing him. His Dad's dead, his Mum's dying and he doesn't seem to have many friends."

Dad looked at Mum and shrugged.

"Your call," he said. "You've met the lad and his mother. What do you think?"

Jesus, now he's a "lad". I think if Dad met Tim he might be somewhat reassured. He hardly looks like a potential suitor.

Mum sighed.

"It's not so much the idea of Anna meeting up with Tim that bothers me," she said, slowly. "It's the idea of her heading into London on her own. I know that Tim knows his way around, but Anna's only been to London once or twice, and that was with us."

Dad nodded.

"I agree," he said. "It sounds like the plan needs some fine-tuning."

Dad always seems to slide into engineering vocabulary when he gets serious.

"Let's get in touch with this chap's mother and see if we can't arrange for them to travel together. One of us could give them a lift to the station and pick them up later on."

"But Dad that's ridiculous. Tim lives miles away but according to him both our trains go into Waterloo. He says it would be really easy to meet there."

But Dad was adamant.

"That may well be the case, but I am not happy with you gallivanting off into central London by yourself. I don't mind putting you onto the train so long as you are with someone, but I am not having you hop onto it based on the off-chance that he will be there to meet you."

Dad stood up and started clearing plates away from the kitchen table.

"Besides," he called over the noise of the kitchen tap, "I'd like to meet this Tim fellow and make sure that he's *compos mentis*."

Mum jumped in.

"According to Tim's mum, he's at the very top of his school's Gifted and Talented register."

"What the hell does that mean?"

"No idea."

Mum and Dad both laughed and started the washing up together.

Apparently, the conversation was finished And like it or not, it seems we had a plan.

The following day was a Friday, and happened to include our last RE lesson before the end of term.

Miss Khan was certainly not the sort of teacher who would bung on a DVD for the whole of the last lesson, so we found ourselves in discussion once again. Fortunately, she had adjusted the seating plan, putting Michael on the other side of the classroom. Harry had been moved also, and in place of the usual two boys Ashley and I found ourselves staring at Martin and David. Unbelievable.

"No doubt she's done the new plan based on ability," hissed Ashley as the two boys settled into their new places. "Two bright kids next to two drongos. It's the latest method. The bright kids are meant to raise the attainment of the weaker ones."

Ashley had always been able to offer endless and alarming insights into the methodology used by classroom teachers. Her mother was Head of English at another school nearby.

Ashley and I watched Martin as he struggled to work out how his new chair fitted under the desk. Ashley sighed.

I nudged her.

"So which of us are the bright pair and which of us are the drongos?"

Ashley snorted.

"I'll leave it to you to decide," she said, airily. She smiled at Martin and David with patronising benevolence and folded her arms in front of her.

Miss Khan set us a task based on the ideas that we had been exposed to last lesson. David and Martin looked at the pile of cards as if they had never seen them before, claiming not to remember any of the quotations. Their blank expressions told us everything we needed to know. Ashley and I settled to the task together, while the two boys flicked small pellets of chewed paper at us across the desk and sniggered.

The task was reasonably simple, so Ashley and I chatted as we worked. She asked me about yesterday's appointment at Moorfield's and I felt compelled to tell her about Tim and our plans to meet up in London the next day.

"So, what's he like?"

"Um. He's clever."

"And?"

"He's into heavy metal."

"Okay! Bit weird. Anything else?"

The question of Tim's looks and physique was hanging in the air, but Ashley was far too high-minded to ask it."

"And I don't fancy him."

"Why not?"

"Trust me, if you saw him you wouldn't have to ask."

Ashley grunted.

"Fair enough. Anything that could be done to improve things? I mean, if I hadn't managed to talk Harry out of his attachment to that man-bracelet then I'm not sure I could ever have seen him as boyfriend material."

"Well, we'd have to talk Tim into drinking build-up shakes for a year, going to the gym, having a new haircut, getting new glasses and re-thinking his entire wardrobe."

Ashley laughed.

"Okay. That does sound like quite a challenge. Even so, though. Don't write him off."

I looked at Ashley and tried to decide how I could explain it to her without sounding quite as shallow as I felt. In the end, I decided to plump for a reasonable amount of honesty and trust that Ashley was a good enough friend to forgive me.

"It's just hard. You know? It seems like ... like nobody else has to contemplate the idea of forcing themselves to be attracted to someone. They just *are* attracted to someone. And then that person's attracted to them. Bingo. Everyone's happy. Game on."

"I think you are seriously overestimating how often that happens. It's not just you that has experienced unrequited love, you know. What Michael did to you was really shitty, but..."

"Actually I'm not sure he *was* being shitty," I interrupted. "To be fair, I misinterpreted some signals. So did you. It's not his fault he's not attracted to me. *I* wouldn't be attracted to me. I get it."

"That's not what you were saying a few days ago."

"I was upset a few days ago. I'm still upset. And I'm not saying I want to be his friend. I'm just not sure he deserves our unremitting hatred."

Ashley scratched her nose. I could tell that she was finding my tendency to hurtle from one extreme of emotion to another a little challenging. Last week I had wanted Michael dead. Preferably castrated first.

I tried to explain.

"Look. I'm just reflecting on the fact that whether I like it or not I can't force Michael to like me. Just like Tim can't force me to like him. Not that I'm assuming he *wants* me to like him. But I get the sneaking feeling that he does. So now ... now ..."

"Now you know you Michael feels?"

"Er. Yes."

Ashley and I worked in silence for the rest of the lesson. The truth is unpleasant sometimes.

Chapter Fifteen

By the time Dad had put us on board the train the next morning, I could tell that he was thoroughly happy with the idea of Tim as my chaperone for the day.

In the half an hour that it took to deliver us both to Woking Station, Tim had revealed his impressive knowledge of London and its history. This was problem solved as far as my Dad was concerned. If a man knew a lot about history, he was irrefutably a sound and practically-minded chap.

I wondered how Boris Johnson fitted into my Dad's little world view, but decided that now was not the time to raise it.

Tim was dressed in another alarming T-shirt, this time sporting a depiction of a band called *Def Leppard*. I didn't examine the image in detail, but it involved a skull and some men wearing tight jeans and bandanas. Enough said.

The T-shirt was tucked in of course, this time into some high-waisted faded blue jeans that were if anything worse than the black ones he wore last week. The Velcro trainers were the same.

Once we were on the train, Tim regaled me with stories. He was quite funny and the conversation flowed surprisingly easily, although I sensed that he was nervous all the same.

It turned out that we were not going to the British Museum or to the National Gallery, but to the Tate Modern instead. Tim explained that it was housed in a converted power station on the Embankment.

"So we won't even need to get the tube," said Tim. "We can be on the Embankment within a couple of minutes from Waterloo."

I didn't know where the Embankment was, but refrained from revealing just how little I seemed to know about the world in comparison with Tim. Instead, I tried to ask some intelligent questions about the gallery.

"What kind of pictures do they have in there?"

"Well, there aren't many actual *pictures*. It's more ... installation based."

I didn't know what this meant either, but didn't say so.

Tim continued with his chatter.

"I thought that since you hadn't been to the London galleries before then the Tate was a better bet than the National or the Portrait. Basically, it's more ... um ... entertaining."

"*Entertaining*?! Doesn't sound like an art gallery to me!"

"Wait and see," said Tim, smiling to himself as he watched the view from the train window.

The Tate Modern was simply extraordinary and Tim was right about the entertainment.

The first thing we saw was a giant crack in the ground floor, reaching from one end of the hall to the other. Someone had actually cut a crack into the concrete floor as a piece of art work. Can you believe it? At one end of the room the crack was tiny, a feather's width. By the time you reached the other end, the crack had widened to several centimetres. People were feeling down into the floor, stretching down, trying to find out how deep it went. Children were running up and down the hall, sometimes joining in with their parents trying to feel as far down into the floor as they could.

Other things that we saw included an extended film of some ants carrying multi-coloured pieces of confetti, strip lights bent into weird shapes and a repetitive film showing a man tripping over a variety of different dogs on street corners. This last one was my favourite.

It was not what I had expected at all and Tim was clearly delighted by my reaction.

"I don't understand," I said, as we stopped to buy a Coke at one of the cafeterias inside the gallery. "I thought that galleries were places where you had to walk around in silence looking at lots of different paintings and nodding wisely."

Tim laughed.

"I think they all used to be like that. Some of

them, to be honest, are still a bit like that. But the Tate Modern is different. The artwork in it is so experimental and bizarre that they have to allow people to react however they wish to."

Tim drained his Coke bottle noisily, then continued.

"My view is that if you find a piece of artwork hilariously funny, then that's how the artwork speaks to you."

"But surely the artists don't want people to be hooting with laughter at their work?"

Tim put the Coke bottle down and wiped his mouth with a paper napkin.

"I am quite sure that most artists would not be offended. They are in the business of creating a reaction in the viewer. That's what art is all about. If your reaction is that you find it hysterically funny, that's as valid a reaction as any."

I thought about some of the po-faced artists that I had seen sometimes on the late-night discussion programmes that Mum and Dad were into. I wasn't too sure that Tim's theory would apply to them.

"Anyway," said Tim. "Enough chat. More art. We haven't even attempted to find any exhibitions for over-18s."

I stared at him, open mouthed.

"They have exhibitions for over-18s?! What the hell is in those?!"

Tim smiled, bowed and waved me towards the door of the cafeteria.

"Madam, this way please."

I didn't have the guts to go into the over-18s section. I was afraid of the very grumpy-looking guard who sat outside the room, scowling at the tourists.

Tim and I loitered around for 20 minutes or so, pretending to look at the display in the adjacent room. Eventually, the guard left his post to go and tell a group of Italian teenagers not to get so close to one of the sculptures. Tim took his chance and dashed in.

Not surprisingly, the guard had returned within a minute and chased Tim out of the room. Tim ran out giggling, and we both got told to leave the gallery.

Tim was still sniggering as we stepped out into the sunshine.

"I've been thrown out of better places than this!" he commented to another guard as we passed him on the door.

The tourists queuing to get into the gallery stared openly.

I folded my arms and looked at Tim.

"This is the first time in my entire life that I have been sent out of a public place," I said. "And it's all your fault."

Tim grinned at me and I couldn't help smiling back.

"Come on," he said. "It's pretty much time to be heading back to the station anyway. There's no way I want us to be late. Annoying a gallery official is one thing, annoying your Dad is quite another."

He pointed back to the route that we had taken from the station.

"Let's have a quick look at the river and then head straight back to Waterloo."

The river was busy as the day was fine. Touring boats filled with Americans cruised up and down the water, and from each one the guide's amplified voice was clearly audible from the bank. We leaned against the railings and watched.

Just as I was opening my mouth to comment on a particularly bored-looking group of tourists, I realised that Tim was laying his right hand over the top of my left one.

I stiffened instantly, but hesitated for a few seconds before gently pulling it away. I kept my eyes fixed on the water.

"Look at those people on the larger boat over there," I said. "They look like they couldn't care less about Christopher Wren and his architecture. Can't say I blame them."

"Anna ..."

"I'm sure they'd rather be sat down in a restaurant somewhere, ordering some food."

"Anna, listen ..."

Finally, I looked at him. He was smiling, which was not what I had expected. I waited for him to say something.

"I know I'm hardly the most exciting romantic prospect, but maybe you would consider thinking about it?"

I couldn't think of a suitable reply, so I said nothing.

"I just think that we have an awful lot in common and maybe we should consider each other as potential partners."

I stared at him. He seemed to be proposing a relationship as if it were some kind of business deal.

"We enjoy each other's company, and you're definitely the most intelligent girl I have ever met."

The air seemed suddenly chilly, and I wanted to go home. I sighed and folded my arms around myself.

"I'm not sure it works like that, Tim. You can't manufacture these things. They just happen."

"Do they? Do they really? You really believe that it's going to happen for you sometime soon?"

I didn't much like the way that this conversation was going, but decided to ignore the slightly vicious undertone in Tim's last remark.

"Well, maybe not soon, but yes. Maybe I do think it will happen. One day."

Tim sighed and looked out across the river.

"I think you may be kidding yourself," he said, flatly. "I'm not sure you will ever meet someone who understands you the way I do."

I felt a surge of anger.

"Tim, you don't even know me. I think it's incredibly arrogant of you to assume that you are my ideal partner at this early stage. Really, I am flattered by your interest, but I would like you to back off, please."

Tim pulled away from the railings and motioned that we should leave.

"Okay. Okay. Point taken. Let's just get going, shall we?"

We walked back to the station and spent most of the return journey in silence.

Chapter Sixteen

I didn't hear from Tim after the day we spent in London. I didn't really know what to do about the situation, so I did nothing. Tim remained on my list of Facebook friends, but we studiously ignored each other. His loss, I told myself, although there was a part of me that wondered whether the loss was equally mine.

The week that followed included all the usual events signalling the end of the school year: endless DVDs, lots of chocolates, the horrors of Sports Day.

Despite the familiarity of these events, the last week had a strange and surreal air for me. At last, and somehow all of a sudden, the day of my surgery was approaching. I had been crossing off the days for what seemed like an eternity, but now the event was just 48 hours away it seemed as if the time had passed in an instant.

Only Ashley, Harry and, inevitably, Michael knew about the surgery. I had always been warned that the date may change, or that the surgery might get cancelled due to another emergency. Somehow

I feared that telling people about it would jinx the event and ensure that it did not happen.

After so many years of waiting, I couldn't bear to think of waiting another minute, let alone another week.

The last day of school seemed to involve a huge amount of clearing up. Miss Khan had enlisted the help of several students to take down all the old displays in her classroom. Mrs. Cameron had not changed the display work for a number of years, and Miss Khan clearly had plans for major changes over the summer.

"I thought I would have quotations from famous religious figures right across this wall here," she said, waving her arms enthusiastically.

"What about non-religious figures?" asked Ashley, who could never resist a debate.

"An interesting idea. So long as the quotations are relevant to the subjects that we cover in Ethics, I have no objection to that. What do you suggest?"

"There's a great one by George Bernard Shaw. Something like the fact that the believer is happier than the atheist is no more significant than the fact that a drunkard is happier than a sober man."

There was a pause. Miss Khan looked at Ashley closely.

"I was not aware of that particular quotation," she said at last. "I shall look it up."

Miss Khan ripped a further strip of poster off the wall, shouting over the sound of tearing paper.

"I suppose his point is to suggest that faith or belief is a state of blissful ignorance."

"Indeed," agreed Ashley. "And he certainly *has* a point."

Miss Khan smiled.

"Personally," she said, "I cannot agree with you. But then I suppose I would say that, being a person of faith."

Miss Khan dumped the latest batch of torn backing paper onto the floor and waggled her finger in Ashley's direction.

"You keep thinking, Ashley. It makes a change to meet a student that applies herself to these ideas. We might make a theologian out of you yet."

She folded her arms and studied Ashley, head on one side.

"Have you thought about RE at A level?"

Ashley and I snorted simultaneously. The idea of Ashley studying religion amused both of us.

"I shall be taking science subjects, Miss Khan. And maths."

"Hmmm. Pity. We lose most of our best thinkers to the sciences. Perhaps that should be telling us something."

Miss Khan looked at me.

"And what about you, Anna?"

"What? RE at A level? Erm ... "

"No, I don't want to have that discussion with you as well. Too depressing for the last day of term. Do you have any suggestions for my wall of inspiring quotations? Make it good, now. You'll be looking at it once a week for another year."

I considered her question, and suddenly the Andrew Marvell poem that we studied in English a few weeks ago came flooding back to me.

"What about: 'At my back I always hear time's winged chariot hurrying near'?"

Miss Khan unfolded her arms and beamed at me.

"I *love* that. It means … well, hang on, you tell me. What do *you* think it means?"

"Um. That when there is so much you want to do and to accomplish in your life, sometimes it feels as if time itself is chasing you."

"Brilliant! I might just have to use that one. Write it down for me, will you? Then get back to helping me with this."

She continued ripping the paper off the wall.

Ashley hissed in my ear while we searched for paper and a pencil in the growing mound of waste.

"So. Are *you* going to tell her that the poem is actually about a bloke trying to get his end away? Or shall I?"

Our last half hour of the year was spent in Form rooms. Most of the clearing up had already been done by now, and Ashley chose this time to present me with a Good Luck card and gifts.

She gave me a box that contained a beautiful old-fashioned teddy bear: to keep me company in the hospital ward, she said.

The card she had painted herself, and she had managed to get almost everyone in the Year to sign it. I was amazed.

"These people don't even know I am going in for surgery. How on earth did you get them all to sign this?"

"I told them that they surely didn't need a reason to do something nice for you. Most of them agreed. Also ..."

"What?"

"I think a lot of them have an idea of what's going on, anyway. I'm afraid that Harry isn't as discreet as I would like him to be."

I laughed.

"That's okay. It's not that I mind people knowing, really. I just had a weird superstitious thing about telling people. Like me saying it out loud would somehow mean it won't happen."

The best part of Ashley's gift was a pile of small, white, sealed envelopes. Each one was labelled with a different day of the week, Monday to Sunday.

"These are for you to open on each one of the days that you are in hospital," she said. "Hopefully there will be something to make you smile inside each of them. I may not be able to be there every day, but I thought that this would be the next best thing."

I held the envelopes in my hands and stood perfectly still. I did not know what to say.

Ashley put her arms around me and hugged me close.

"You will be all right, Anna," she whispered. "You'll be fit before you know it and back to your old self. Everything is going to be just fine."

I nodded as we pulled apart.

"And with a bit of luck, I'll even be able to face the world without being stared at."

Ashley has always been dubious about the idea that this surgery will work a miracle. I saw a flicker of doubt pass across her face as she registered my optimistic remark.

"Maybe," she said at last, and smiled at me reassuringly. "Now make sure you look after that bear."

Chapter Seventeen

It wasn't until my first night in hospital that it occurred to me I had anything to be scared about.

The Ward Sister showed me that I would be in a private room next to the Nurses' Station.

"It means we can keep a really close eye on you," she said, warmly.

"Oh," I said. "Right."

"You will probably come straight back here after the surgery, but there is a chance that we might pop you into Intensive Care. Just for a night."

I swallowed.

"Really? Why?"

She smiled encouragingly.

"Purely because there we can keep an *even closer* eye on you!"

"And what will you be looking for?" I asked, cautiously, unsure whether I really wanted to know.

She flapped her hands dismissively.

"Just making sure that your breathing and everything else is totally fine. Nothing for you to worry about at all."

It clearly *was* something that any sane person should be worried about, but I decided to accept her platitudes rather than to go down the route of full-on panic at this stage.

"So if you'd like to settle in, the anaesthetist will coming to visit you soon."

This was news to me.

"Why do I need to meet with the anaesthetist?"

The Nurse started to bustle around the room, straightening the blankets, plumping the pillows and fiddling with the overhead lighting.

"We always make sure that the anaesthetist visits any patient whose surgery is particularly ... um ... well ..."

Serious? Dangerous? A bloody terrible idea?

"... not *purely routine.*"

Shit. The euphemisms were really flowing now.

The Nurse left me to settle into the room so I sat on the bed, unsure what to do. It seemed ridiculous to get into my pyjamas at this stage, but it seemed almost as ridiculous not to, when all the other patients were wandering around in bedclothes.

A grey bedside cabinet made of metal and plastic stood next to the bed. The top shelf was for some reason hidden behind miniature saloon-style swing doors, while the cupboard underneath was more conventional. I stored Ashley's pile of sealed envelopes carefully behind the saloon doors and put my wash-bag in the cupboard.

I checked my phone. No new text messages, although my Facebook notifications said that several people had written on my wall.

Harry: Good luck, Anna!

Elaine: See you next term, Anna. Looking forward to it!

She probably can't wait to have a nose.

Jeanette: Get well soon! RE would be really crap without you.

Good to know that some of my contributions to RE have provided Jeanette with some entertainment. I wondered whether she was referring to the Mrs. Cameron incident, but decided that this was probably paranoia. Jeanette wasn't that bad, really.

Michael: Get well soon, Anna. And sorry about everything. Please stay in touch. x

Much to my annoyance, just for a moment my heart did skip a beat. Michael.

Who knows whether his desire to stay in touch was genuine after everything that had happened. We will have to wait and see. Somehow it seemed a little less important right now.

I stowed my phone away behind the saloon-doors and looked around the room.

The walls were painted pale blue. Several chips were knocked out of the paintwork, and the far corner housed a grubby-looking basin. The walls were covered with various laminated hospital posters reminding staff to wash their hands, to pull certain levers in a particular direction, or to dial a range of numbers. A plastic visitor's chair waited patiently next to the bed.

A tap at the open door made me jump. Standing in the doorway was a slim, dark-haired man of average height. He wore metal-rimmed glasses and the dark, slightly hollow-eyed look of a tired Doctor at the end of a long shift.

He was dressed in a checked shirt and Chinos. The obligatory stethoscope, the trademark of the hospital doctor, was slung around his neck. In his right hand he carried a clipboard.

"Hello, Anna. My name is Dr. Stevenson. I'm your anaesthetist for tomorrow. Is it all right if I come in and talk to you?"

This was probably the first time that any Doctor had asked my permission to do anything without being halfway through doing it already. I was going to like this one.

Dr. Stevenson settled himself into the plastic visitor's chair next to my bed.

"Bit of a crap room, isn't it?" he said, pushing his glasses further up his nose and smiling at me.

"It's okay I guess. Better than being on the main bit of the ward."

Dr. Stevenson shook his head.

"Wait until you've been here a few days. You'll be desperate to get out there and see some other patients."

He waved his hand in the general direction of the Ward.

"There's all manner of entertainment out there once you're fit enough to enjoy it. Trust me."

I already did.

"So. Anna. I'm going to need to ask you a few questions; but more importantly, you can ask me anything you like as well. Anything at all."

"Okay."

"Let's start with your own health. Do you have or have you ever suffered from asthma?"

"No."

"Any other breathing difficulties?"

"No."

"Heart problems?"

I sighed.

"Not that I am aware of."

He smiled and rested his clip board back onto his knees.

"You'd think that we'd know all this by now, the amount of time we've spent poking our noses into your business, wouldn't you? Sorry this is so tedious, Anna."

Dr. Stevenson worked through his list of questions as swiftly as he could, and from that moment I didn't mind a bit. In fact, I was enjoying his attention. After he had finished, he sat back in his chair and stretched his hands behind his head.

"Boy, it's been a long day," he said.

I nodded.

"Now it's your turn, Anna. Is there anything you would like to ask about tomorrow?"

"Um. Yes."

Dr. Stevenson waited.

"You're probably going to think that this is ridiculous."

"Go on."

"Last year I saw this Documentary programme on BBC2. It was about patients who had experienced being awake during surgery. I mean, they were conscious, but they couldn't move or say anything. Some of them said that they had suffered terrible pain during the procedure. Most of the Doctors and Nurses didn't believe them, and said that they had been dreaming."

I paused and looked closely at Dr. Stevenson. He was still sat with his hands behind his head, listening politely.

"So what I want to know is ... is it true? And if it *is* true, how do you know that it's not going to happen to me tomorrow?"

There. I had said it. The fear that had been haunting me ever since I had seen that God-damned programme. Most of the time I had pushed it out of my mind, but occasionally it came bobbing back, usually in the middle of the night.

Dr. Stevenson unfolded his arms and leaned forward.

"Okay, Anna. I am aware of the Documentary and I am sorry it frightened you. Perhaps I can reassure you."

I certainly hoped so.

"While awareness during anaesthesia does sometimes happen, it is very rare indeed."

"Not good enough. *Very rare indeed* means it still happens."

"Hang on! I haven't finished yet!"

"Sorry."

"The vast majority of cases occur during surgery when a very light anaesthetic is used for some reason – because the patient has heart problems, which you don't, or because the patient is having a Caesarean section to remove a baby, which you're not … unless I've got entirely the wrong case notes in front of me!"

I couldn't help laughing, despite my anxiety.

"Anna, I don't want to give you an entirely different cause for alarm, but … you do realise that the anaesthetic that I am going to be giving you is … well … pretty hefty?"

"What do you mean?"

"Well. No-one's probably shared this with you, but you seem like a sensible girl who would prefer to know the facts. Your operation is going to take at least eight hours. Maybe more. The surgeons will work in shifts. I will have an assistant who will be able to provide me with breaks during the procedure, but I will be on-hand at all times. I promise."

I stared at him.

"*Eight hours?!*"

"As I said. Maybe more."

He let this register for a while.

"So believe me, the amount of anaesthesia I'm going to be pumping into you … you're *not* going to wake up during the surgery!"

"Right. Point taken."

"Happy?"

"Delighted. It all sounds wonderful."

Dr. Stevenson winked at me and grinned.

He was the only Doctor I had ever met who seemed to get my sarcastic back-chat. I found myself wondering whether he was married.

"So, now I've given you all sorts of things to worry about, let's make sure that you don't lie awake all night doing exactly that."

Dr. Stevenson picked up the chart at the end of my bed and filled in one of the columns.

"I am prescribing you a sedative for tonight. Please agree to take it when the nurse offers it to you. It will make sure that you get some rest rather than lie awake all night fretting."

"Okay. Sounds like good advice."

Dr. Stevenson hung the chart back onto the end of the bed and smiled at me.

"I will look forward to seeing you in the morning, Anna."

Chapter Eighteen

The sedative didn't work.

I spent much of the night listening to the hushed but constant babble between the Nurses at their station. They offered to close the door but I asked them to leave it. I found listening to their mundane gossip strangely comforting, a distraction from the more threatening thoughts inside my head.

The sedative did make me extremely groggy, and the nurses had warned me to ask for help if I got up to go to the loo. I ignored them, of course. But as I found myself swaying from side to side in the bathroom, questioning my ability to return to my bed, I realised that they had been right.

When the Nurses' conversations subsided in the early hours of the morning, I tried listening to some music. Nothing seemed quite right, and nothing provided the distraction that I wanted.

In the end I listened to the breathing of restless patients in the Ward surrounding me. Some were snoring, others was grumbling in the fitful state between sleep and wakefulness. Occasionally a light would appear on the Nurses' Station and one of them would get up to attend to a patient's request.

"God, it's Mrs. Jackson again. You go this time, she prefers you."

"Okay. But we take it in turns. She's bound to claim that she needs the loo at least twice more before the shift is over."

At around 4.30am, the fingers of dawn started to stretch across the room. It felt like I had not slept at all, although I suppose I must have done.

Within an hour or so the Nurses were busy, preparing to hand over to the morning shift and rousing some of the patients for their first medication of the day. I was included in the drugs round and a Nurse appeared next to my bed holding two yellow capsules in a small plastic beaker.

"What are those?" I asked, dubiously.

"It's a pre-med."

"A what?"

"A pre-med. We ask patients to take this an hour before they go down to surgery. It helps you to relax and not to worry about anything. Once you've taken it, *do not* go to the loo by yourself. I mean it this time, Anna."

"Okay, okay."

I took the pills.

Within 20 minutes my head was swimming and my vision was blurred. What the hell was in those things? Part of me felt outraged, part of me couldn't summon the energy to care about anything at all.

I must have dozed off, because the next thing I remember I was on a trolley and being wheeled down the corridor.

"All right, Missy?"

A hugely fat man was pushing the trolley. He was jovial and no-nonsense in his approach to the job.

"We're going for a little ride," he said.

The trolley trundled along the corridor, swaying round corners and nosing its way through swing-doors.

"It's like a fairground ride. Ghost Train," I said randomly to the fat man at the end. He smiled indulgently.

What the hell was the matter with me? It wasn't a bit like a Ghost Train. What a stupid thing to say.

A rising tide of panic surged through my chest. Did this man even know which surgeon I was meant to be delivered to? This is ridiculous. In fact, the whole thing is ridiculous. Am I really about to let these people cut me open for no good reason? There's nothing wrong with me!

That's it. I've changed my mind. I shouldn't have to face this just because the rest of society can't walk past me without staring. They're the ones with the problem, not me.

As soon as I saw the Doctors I would tell them that I had made a mistake and wanted to go home. Simple.

"Here we are, Missy. I'll be leaving you now. See you in a few hours, maybe."

What did he mean, "maybe". Jesus. I had to get out of here.

"Hello, Anna."

Dr. Stevenson's face was barely visible behind a huge green mask. I recognised his eyes, his glasses and his voice.

I tried to open my mouth to say something to him, to start voicing my change of heart, but I found that I couldn't.

Two nursing assistants fussed around me and I realised suddenly that a needle was going into my left hand.

"Just fitting a cannula here, Anna. Won't take a second."

I lay there helplessly while a tube was inserted into my vein. Time was hurtling by and it felt like I was watching the scene from behind soundproof glass. I hollered my objections, but no-one heard me.

"The first drugs are going in now, Anna, and I want you to start counting down from twenty. Can you do that for me?"

I found myself obeying mechanically.

"Twenty. Nineteen. Eighteen. Seventeen. Sixteen. Fift ..."

Chapter Nineteen

White light. Noise.

Wasn't I meant to be counting? Where had I got to?

I recognised the distinctive Australian accent of my chief surgeon telling me that it was all right as he stuffed a rigid plastic tube up my nose. It wasn't all right. It hurt. I fought him and two Nurses held me down. I tried to call out but I realised that my jaws were wired together. How had that happened?

Then blackness.

The early phase of my recovery passed in a fitful haze of hot, white waves of nausea and disorientation.

I struggled to breathe much of the time. I sat propped up against hospital pillows, rigid with terror that each breath would fail me. I stared at the ceiling.

Nurses, Doctors and my parents faded in and out of my vision over what seemed like hours, days, weeks ... ? Who knows. Somehow, time had ceased to exist.

Ashley's envelopes lay unopened behind the little swing-doors. Neither of us had realised that I would not be able to do anything other than concentrate on drawing breath for what turned out to be three whole days.

The fourth day dawned at last through a tenuous veil of normality. Cautiously, I lowered my eyes from the ceiling and took in my surroundings for the first time since I had left on a trolley.

Same dingy little room. Same grubby little basin. Lots of new machines, all of which were attached to me by various bits of tubing. A tube up my nose, two tubes in my face, a tube in my side, God knows what else.

Clearly I was to be stuck in this bed for some time to come.

I turned gingerly towards the side cupboard and opened the saloon-doors. I was unsure what day it was but it didn't seem to matter now.

I opened Monday's envelope and started to read the contents.

Dear Anna

So, your first day! I hope that you have settled in and that they haven't woken you up too early. My Nan says that in hospital they wake you up at night to give you a sleeping pill, and then wake you up at 5am to start the breakfasts. Sounds horrendous to me...

Ashley's chatter was wonderfully soothing. I imagined her voice as I read her words. By the time I had read most of Monday's envelope, a Nurse came in and informed me that it was Thursday. She seemed pleased with how much better I was.

"Your friends were hoping to come and visit this afternoon," she said. "I shall let your Dad know that would be fine. Your Mum and Dad have been here every day so far, although I'm not sure how much you've been aware of."

I didn't even know what bloody day of the week it was, let alone how often I had been visited.

"One of your friends turned up on Tuesday morning and sat with you for ages. They left when your parents arrived."

That must have been Ashley. How lovely. I felt sad that I had not been aware of her being there.

"Your Dad thought that he and your Mum would come later in the evening today, so you could see your friends this afternoon. We don't like too many people to be in here at once."

She fiddled for a while with the various tubes, machines and bags of fluid that surrounded me, then surveyed me critically.

"Do you want a pad of paper and a pen for now? You'll learn to speak through those wires after a while, but you might find it easier to write things down in the meantime."

I nodded gratefully.

The Nurse brought me the paper and a pen and I managed my first word of communication in days.

Thanks.

The nurse turned to go but I tapped the pen against the pad of paper to stop her.

"Yes, Anna? Was there something else?"

I wrote on the pad again.

I would like a mirror. I haven't seen myself yet.

The nurse looked anxious.

"Anna, I will bring you a mirror, but I need you to be prepared for what you will see. You do realise that you are very swollen and bruised? That you have tubes coming of you, and that much of you is covered up with a dressing?"

I nodded and tapped my pen against my written request.

The nurse left the room.

I looked down at my left hand. The cannula was still in place, much of it held down by surgical tape. The skin on the back of my hand was varying shades of black, purple and yellow. The human body doesn't take too kindly to having needles stuck into it.

The nurse reappeared holding a makeup mirror. She perched on the bed next to me and patted my right hand.

"Ready?" she asked.

I nodded.

"Here you go then," she said, and gently passed me the mirror.

I looked at my reflection and the prototype version of my new face looked back at me. Tinges of purple were apparent across much of it, and my cheeks and jawline were puffy. I touched my own cheek in disbelief.

The nurse started to babble.

"This is very early days, Anna. Things will improve so dramatically with every single day, you'll see. The swelling will go down, the bruises will fade, soon you won't know yourself ..."

I held out my hand towards her and waved it slightly to stop her speaking. I then reached for the pen again.

I can't believe how good it looks already. It's a miracle.

The nurse was delighted.

"Oh Anna, you had me worried there! I am so pleased you can see through all the medical paraphernalia and all the swelling. You're right. It *is* wonderful. Dr. Poole is a genius. You're going to look simply amazing. It will just take a little bit more time, that's all."

Ashley and Harry arrived in the early afternoon. Ashley's instinct was to come over and hug me but I waved her away and then pointed to the pad of paper on which I wrote:

Too many tubes. Too sore.

Harry left the room to find a second chair, while Ashley sat down and patted my arm.

"It's so great to see you, Anna. We've been thinking about you every day."

I scribbled on the pad.

I guess I look a lot better than I did before!

Ashley squeezed my arm.

"Oh Anna, it's far too early to tell. You're all swollen

and bruised; it's impossible for me to see what you'll look like yet."

I shook my head and scribbled again.

No. I mean better than I did on Tuesday! I don't even remember you being here. I must have looked awful.

Ashley looked puzzled.

"I don't understand. I didn't come to see you on Tuesday. Neither did Harry. Your Dad said that we had to wait until the hospital were sure it was okay. They didn't want too many people pestering you in the first three days because you were so poorly."

I paused for a moment before I wrote on the pad again.

Michael?

I sincerely hoped that Michael *hadn't* come to see me when I was in such a hideous state, so it was a relief when Ashley shook her head.

"I doubt it. Harry and I had a word with him, To be honest, Anna, we told him to stay away from you – at least for now. I didn't think that his presence would aid your recovery. I hope that's okay."

I nodded gratefully. Ashley did tend to get things right. Most of the time.

Harry reappeared at the doorway, holding a bright green plastic chair and grinning.

"This place is full of nutters!" he said. "I've just had this old woman ask me when it's tea time."

He set the chair down next to Ashley and settled into it.

"So," he said, amiably. "What's it been like?"

I picked up the pen again.

Horrendous. Today's the first day that I've had a clue what's going on.

"Somebody came to visit Anna on Tuesday and we're trying to work out who it was," said Ashley. "There's no way it could have been Michael, could it?"

Harry shook his head firmly.

"Definitely not. He actually agreed with us that visiting Anna was not a good idea just yet. I think he was relieved to be honest. I'd be very surprised if he had changed his mind."

The Nurse came in to check my tubes again. She nodded at Ashley and Harry before setting to work.

"So who the hell was it, I wonder?" Ashley frowned.

Harry shrugged and looked at me.

"I wouldn't have thought that anyone else from school would have had the initiative. It's only because we rang your Dad that we knew which hospital you were in, let alone which Ward to find you on."

The Nurse loosened a valve on one of the machines that surrounded me and then tapped me on the shoulder.

"Are you trying to work out who it was that came to visit you, Anna? I can find out if you like. We keep records."

I nodded and gave her a *thumbs up* sign.

She padded out of the room, her white rubber-soled shoes squelching on the polished floor. Through the door I could just about make out that she was opening a filing cabinet next to the Nurses' Station.

"Blimey," said Harry. "It's like MI5 in here."

"Don't be melodramatic, Harry. Of *course* they have to keep records. It's ... it's obvious."

"So obvious that you thought to ask the Nurse straight away. Oh, actually, no you didn't."

Ashley pursed her lips together and refused to grace his comments with an answer.

The Nurse returned holding an open cardboard file and flapping a sheet of paper.

"It was someone called Tim Stademan. I remember him now. Skinny boy. *Guns n Roses* T-shirt. Took me right back to the early 90s. You're too young to remember them. So's he, so I've no idea why he was wearing them on his T-shirt."

She left the room again, humming.

I looked at Ashley. Her eyebrows were raised high and she was smiling.

"So!" she said. "Now we know."

I nodded.

"You must admit – it was nice of him to go to all that trouble. He's only just met you and he came to visit you in hospital. That's really lovely."

Ashley nudged Harry, who nodded immediately.

"Yeah. This guy sounds like he must be all right. You should introduce us when you're a bit better."

I nodded glumly.

I supposed they must be right that it was kind of Tim to come and visit me.

But the truth was, I felt a little violated.

Chapter Twenty

I did not see Michael until I was back at home, a full ten days after Ashley and Harry had visited me. He came over on his bike on a Sunday afternoon and tapped on the door. My Mum seemed surprised to see him.

"Michael! What a nice surprise. We haven't seen you for ages. How's that mischievous dog of yours?"

I heard Michael chatting politely to my Mum as she showed him through to the conservatory at the back of the house. I was sitting in the sunniest spot reading a book. Bingo the cat was curled up next to me, feigning sleep through slitted eyes.

Michael sat down in the chair opposite me. He looked nervous.

"How are you feeling, Anna?"

I had learned to talk by now. Although my jaws were wired together, teeth clamped tightly shut, it was possible to articulate quite clearly with my lips.

"I'm okay. Taking one day at a time. I get very tired."

Michael stared at me for a few seconds. It seemed like he was trying to decide what to say.

"I didn't realise that you wouldn't be able to open your mouth," he said at last. "How do you ... how do you eat and drink?"

"Drinking isn't a problem, the liquid goes between my teeth. Eating has to be the same, so all I can have is plain soups. I've mainly been living off these."

I showed him a packet of Complan, an energy shake designed for elderly people and invalids.

He took the packet and examined it carefully. I noticed that his hands were shaking slightly. I wondered why he was so anxious. After a while he put the packet down.

"I ... I had no idea."

"No idea about what?"

"That ... that it would be like this."

"Like what? What do you mean?"

Michael rubbed his left hand across his forehead and pushed his hair out of his eyes.

"That you would have to live like this. That you would look so ... so pale. That it would take this long."

I shrugged and said nothing.

"Ashley says you have to live like this for *six weeks*. Is that true?"

"That's the minimum. It might be longer. Possibly up to eight or nine weeks. It depends how quickly the bones knit together."

Michael nodded. He looked miserable.

I sighed.

"Michael, I don't know what you were expecting; but it is okay, you know. I'm getting better. Slowly."

Michael nodded again.

"This was my choice, anyway. I wanted the surgery. It's my only chance to have something resembling a normal life. I know I look pretty weird right now, but the Doctors are pleased with how the operation went. They say that my face will look much more symmetrical once the swelling has gone down. They hope that my appearance could be almost normal."

Michael cracked his knuckles. I have always hated it when he does that.

"There was nothing wrong with the way you looked before."

I folded my arms and raised my eyebrows at him.

"I think you and I both know that's a lie."

"It's not a lie. It's my opinion. I liked you the way you were."

"No you didn't. That much was obvious."

Michael cracked his knuckles again and looked even more miserable.

"Anna ... I really am sorry about that night. At the party? I am so sorry that I hurt your feelings. I never meant to."

"I know that, Michael. It's okay. Honestly. It doesn't matter."

"It *does* matter. I've been over and over it. I must have done something to confuse you; led you on in some way."

I felt weary already.

"Michael, forget about it. I really don't want to go over this any more."

"Well I do. I'm ... I'm moving back to Hindhead in a few days and I want to set the record straight. I don't want to leave while there is bad feeling between us."

"There isn't any bad feeling! Look, Michael, I hate to puncture your self-image but I have actually moved on from that night. I've had slightly more important things to be focusing on."

"I know that. I'm not trying to suggest I'm so wonderful that ... that you'll never get over it. I just need to explain. So we can both move on."

I sighed.

"Go on, then."

"The truth is, Anna, that while it is the case that I don't see you in that way ... "

"Thanks for spelling it out again."

"Let me finish. While that is true ... it's also true that I don't really see *anyone* in that way. I'm not really ... um ... interested in anyone."

"You're not trying to tell me that you're gay are you?"

"No! No. Nothing like that."

"Because it's fine. I wouldn't have a problem with it."

"I'm not gay! It's not like that."

"Well how is it then?"

"I ... I just want you to know that me not being interested in you was nothing to do with you as such. I just ... I don't really feel like that about anyone right now. I don't know why."

I examined his face closely. His expression looked genuine, yet what he was saying seemed totally ludicrous. Suddenly, I felt simply exhausted and I just wanted him to go home.

"Look, Michael, I really appreciate what you're trying to do but it honestly isn't necessary. If you must know, there's someone else in my life right now, anyway."

Michael looked surprised.

"Oh really? I didn't know that."

"Yes. His name's Tim. We met a few weeks ago and he's really keen. He took me into London for the day. He also came to visit me in hospital."

"That's great, Anna. Really. I'm happy for you. You deserve it more than anyone."

I didn't even like Tim, but somehow I was making him out to be some kind of romantic love-god. What on earth was I thinking?

Michael stood up and stretched his arms above his head. His T-shirt rode up over his torso to reveal a taut, brown abdomen and the top band of his Calvin Klein underwear. I felt a twinge of desire, which I hastily pushed aside.

"I'd better get going," said Michael, yawning. He seemed suddenly relaxed, like his old self. He looked at me and smiled.

"We're moving on Wednesday," he said. "Dad's been offered a better job back at his old company. Mum has always wanted to go back to Hindhead, so we're going to rent in the area until she finds us a house. Dad says he doesn't care where we live, so long as Mum stops moaning."

I nodded. Strangely, I didn't really feel anything about Michael leaving. Neither sad nor relieved. It just didn't seem to matter any more.

"So can we keep in touch?" Michael said, hesitantly. "Chat online occasionally?"

"Sure. Of course."

"And Hindhead's not that far away. Maybe we could all meet up sometime."

"Absolutely," I said. "We'll do that."

I think we both knew that our "friendship" was destined to exist only in the world of Facebook from now on. The suggestion of meeting up was just one of those things that you say to make your last face-to-face meeting less embarrassing.

"Right. I'm off. Say goodbye to your Mum for me?"

"I will."

"And good luck with Tim. Sounds like you've met someone really nice."

I said nothing. Michael turned and walked away, raising his hand in a farewell gesture as he did so.

I knew that I would never see him again.

Chapter Twenty-One

Just as Michael slid out of my life, so Tim found his way in, and both of these changes seemed to happen with the same sense of inevitability.

My parents were impressed that Tim had taken the initiative to find out where I was and to visit me in the hospital. They were keen for me to invite him to our house and since it was impossible to explain my reluctance to do so, that is what happened.

He arrived at the appointed time on a Thursday afternoon. The T-shirt of the day advertised a band called *Led Zeppelin* and listed all the venues on their 1977 US tour. I refrained from commenting and invited him in. Just inside the door he stopped and removed his trainers.

"You don't need to bother," I said, feeling irritated already.

"I don't mind," he replied, continuing with the process. "It's what I'm used to. Feels weird if I don't. Mum always insists on no shoes in the house, as she doesn't like the idea of street dirt in the carpet. She thinks it's unhygienic."

Tim padded through the kitchen in his grey school socks and followed me into the conservatory.

"Wow," he said. "This house is amazing. How long have you lived here?"

I considered this as we sat down.

"Um. About ten or eleven years, I guess. I was born in West London but we moved out here when I was four or five."

"Do you remember living in London?"

"Not really. Snippets of the house. The wallpaper in my room. The French windows in the living room. Little things like that. I certainly don't remember London itself."

"Whereabouts did you live?"

"Ealing."

"Uhuh. Hmmm."

"What's that supposed to mean?"

"Nothing. I'm just not surprised that you said Ealing, that's all. You were hardly likely to say Tottenham or Brixton."

"Why not?"

Tim waved his hand around, indicating the surroundings.

"Because clearly your parents have a lot of money."

I felt inexplicably insulted by this, but could not think of a suitable reply. I paused.

"And your parents ... um ... don't? Didn't. Or rather ... you know what I mean."

"No. We never had money, but since Dad died we've had even less. He didn't have any kind of life insurance, presumably because like most people he didn't plan on dying so young. We also didn't know that Mum had MS at the time."

"Really? Oh."

"She'd been getting symptoms but the GP kept on saying that her tiredness and the tingling in her arms and legs were all down to stress. She suffers with stress and anxiety, so that seemed to make sense. But then she was diagnosed with MS four days after Dad died."

"Jesus. How awful."

"I know. Something of a shit week, eh?!"

I didn't really know what to say to this, so I said nothing.

"Anyway," said Tim, briskly. "Don't know why we're talking about that, I'm here to see you. How are you feeling? You look considerably better than the last time I saw you!"

I nodded.

"I'm okay," I said, and then hesitated. "Um. Thanks. For coming to visit me in hospital, I mean. You didn't need to. Especially after ... after our day in London."

Tim flapped his hands again, this time in a gesture of dismissal.

"Nonsense. I wanted to come and see you. I wanted to make sure that you were okay. I didn't think that you were aware of me being there."

"I wasn't. The nurse told me two days later that you had visited."

"Ah. I see."

Silence descended upon the room, punctuated only by the ticking of our old Victorian clock that stood in the hallway. Bingo tiptoed across the conservatory and slunk into the shade of the living room.

A tap at the front door made both of us jump.

"That'll be Ashley and Harry," I said, standing up.

Tim looked slightly crestfallen.

"I didn't know that you had invited anyone else," he said. "Who are Ashley and Harry?"

"Ashley's my best friend and Harry's her boyfriend. He's a really good friend of mine, too."

"Right."

I had not wanted to spend the afternoon alone with Tim and Ashley had been desperate to meet him anyway, so persuading her to come over with Harry had not been difficult. Our idea was to play board games, and Harry arrived carrying Cluedo and Monopoly under his arm.

"I vote Monopoly," he said, placing the games on the coffee table in front of us. "I feel like a bit of financial speculation."

I shrugged.

"I don't mind," I said. "This is Tim, by the way. Tim, meet Harry and Ashley."

Tim did his silly little mock bow.

"Which game would *you* prefer, Tim?" said Ashley, magnanimously.

Tim scratched his chin, thoughtfully.

"Well," he said. "Monopoly holds the attraction of

giving all of you a right Royal thrashing. I happen to be particularly good at Monopoly."

Harry slapped his hand down onto the lid of the box.

"Right! That settles it. We can't ignore a thrown gauntlet like that, folks. Monopoly it is. But I warn you now, Tim ... I have no morals when it comes to buying up vast numbers of hotels."

"You'll need to win some money first," said Tim. "Bring it on."

And so it was. Harry and Tim were chipping each other like old mates while Ashley and I looked on in amazement. Only boys could be so instantly at ease with one another. Ashley says we could learn a lot from them, and I must admit that she is probably right.

The game lasted all afternoon and the banter continued. I certainly had not laughed so much since I had come out of hospital, indeed at times I wished I could stop because my stitches were sore. It was worth it though; it felt so good to laugh again.

As the game was drawing to a conclusion, Mum came into the conservatory and invited my friends to stay for supper.

"Anna won't be able to join in with the eating part of it, I'm afraid! But she's got used to joining us at the table with one of her Complan shakes, haven't you, Anna?"

"Hmmm. What exciting flavour shall I choose this evening, out of the four on offer?" I mused.

Harry clutched his stomach and groaned.

"God, Anna. It must be awful. Aren't you ... you know ... *starving* all the time?"

"Not everyone is quite such a monumental piglet as you," Ashley pointed out.

I laughed.

"You get used to it," I said. "The worst thing is sometimes I totally forget. I'll smell what's cooking for supper and think it smells appetising, then suddenly I remember that I won't be eating it."

Harry shuddered. I continued.

"The worst days are Fridays, when we usually get Fish and Chips. Mum and Dad don't get it at the moment, as they realise that would just be torture for me. But last Friday I felt happy that it was Fish and Chip night for a good five seconds before I remembered that I can't eat! It's weird."

Ashley and Harry packed the game away, while Tim offered to help Mum lay the table; I could tell she was impressed. I stayed on the sofa with the cat. There have to be some advantages to my current situation, and being exempt from household chores is definitely one of them.

Mum produced lasagne for supper, a meal which I don't really like. She is being brilliant about avoiding all my favourite meals, although she says that she is going to run out of my pet hates before too long. I am not so sure. I have always been a faddy eater.

Ashley, Harry and Tim seemed more than happy with the food, and tucked into it with gusto. I sipped on my vanilla-flavoured shake and tried not to feel envious. I have a recurring fantasy about biting into a piece of really crusty bread. When you haven't been able to open your mouth for weeks, you'd be surprised just how much you miss the sensation of biting.

Ashley reported the latest on her cat, which had now produced its kittens. Their appearance clearly evidenced the fact that Minky the Siamese was the father, although his owners denied hotly that they had left it a little late to have him neutered.

"It's ridiculous," said Ashley between mouthfuls. "I think they're confusing their cat with a wayward teenage son – like we're going to demand Child Support payments from him! All my Mum wants is some help to find homes for the kittens."

"And it's not as if your Mum is in a position to blame them for not getting their cat neutered early enough," said Harry. "She didn't have your cat done, and bingo! Look at the result!"

Bingo, who had joined us at the foot of the table, pricked up his ears at the sound of his name and mewed silently. He's a bit like a dog, really.

Ashley nodded.

"I know. Mum's useless with stuff like that. She just never gets round to it."

Dad looked a little pained at Ashley's casual dismissal of her own mother's competency. He changed the subject.

"So. Tim. Been into London again recently? Visited any museums?"

Tim wiped his mouth on a napkin.

"Um, not recently. Mum hasn't been too well."

"Oh. I'm sorry to hear that. What's been the matter with her? There are a lot of nasty bugs flying around this summer, I must say ..."

Mum leapt in before Dad could continue.

"Tim's mother has Multiple Sclerosis, darling. You remember I told you? She has good days and bad days, isn't that right Tim?"

Tim nodded.

"More bad than good recently, I'm afraid. She's pretty much lost the use of both her hands now, so I have to do most things for her whenever the Carer's not around."

The rest of us sat and absorbed this information. Eventually, Mum broke the silence.

"If there's anything we can do, Tim, you will let us know? I would hate to think of you struggling on your own. You've done so much for Anna, the least we can do is to lend a hand if we can."

I felt slightly resentful at Mum's implication. I wasn't aware that Tim had done "so much" for me. Tim seemed to agree.

"I really haven't done anything, Mrs. Jones. I see Anna because I like her. No reason other than that."

He looked at me, shyly.

I felt myself turning red. Ashley and Harry were beaming at me from across the table. My heart sank.

Why did everyone seem so convinced of Tim's excellence as a candidate for my affections? Everyone, that is, except me.

Chapter Twenty-Two

Ashley phoned me that night when I was already in bed. She said that she wanted to talk.

"Okay. What about?"

"Tim."

I sighed. I should have known.

"What about Tim?"

"I liked him."

"Yes I sensed that."

"Harry liked him too."

"Yes. That was obvious."

"So both of us *really* liked him."

"Yes."

There was a silence for several seconds.

"Anna, I don't know why you're being like this."

"Like what?"

"Like *this*. Non-committal. Monosyllabic. Downright sniffy."

"*Sniffy?!*"

"Sniffy."

"Well I'm sorry. I don't mean to be."

"What do *you* think about Tim now that you have seen him again?"

I groaned. I truly did not want to have this conversation again.

"I don't know. About the same as I did before. He's bright. He's interesting in lots of ways. He's a little bit full-on. And ... and I do not fancy him. There is nothing I can do about that."

"You honestly don't think that it's worth giving him a chance?"

"What do you mean by "giving him a chance"? You keep saying these things that don't make any sense. What should I be doing, exactly? Letting him feel me up? He'd have to mind the stitches."

"Don't be ridiculous. Of course not. I'm not talking about anything like that, especially not at the moment while you are recovering from surgery. The idea would be ludicrous."

"Well *what* then?"

"I mean that now might be a good time to just ... to just *open your mind* up a little bit."

"Uh oh. There's a definite whiff of Oprah coming through again."

"Anna, if you start the Oprah Winfrey accusations again I shall quite honestly scream."

"Sorry. I'm all ears."

"My point is that now I have seen you with Tim, I can tell that you're putting barriers up. You're so determined that he is not right for you and you've written him off, just like that. The poor boy doesn't stand a chance. Do you see what I mean?"

"Not really. Look. You didn't come to London with us. He was really quite ... *pushy*. In the way that he asked me out, I mean. He actually implied that someone like me couldn't do any better."

"Really? I didn't realise that."

"No. Because I didn't tell you. Because it's not necessarily any of your business. But since you're so determined that he is my ideal lover, perhaps it's time you knew a few home truths."

"Okay then."

"Tim made a pass at me and when I politely ignored it he made a little speech about how he felt we were suited."

"Right. Go on."

"He pointed out that we get on and have things in common. I'm not so sure about that, but certainly we had had a good day in London and up to that point I had enjoyed his company."

"So what's the problem?"

"The *problem*, quite aside from the fact that I truly don't fancy him, which no-one seems to want to accept, is that he then got quite ... well ... *pushy*, as I said. I can't think of another word for it. He wasn't exactly nasty, but he did imply that I was kidding myself by hoping for someone better."

"Don't forget that he would have been smarting from the rejection at that point, so presumably he was just lashing out. I wouldn't take what he said too seriously."

"You don't think that it revealed a nasty streak in him? Or revealed that deep down he doesn't think very much of me?"

"No I don't. It's perfectly obvious that he thinks a great deal of you. I think he was just feeling defensive and he handled it badly. You can't hold someone to account for every single word that they say in every single situation."

"Well you've changed your tune."

"What's that supposed to mean?"

"Just a few weeks ago, a certain teacher lost her job because you reported her for nothing more than a few badly-chosen words."

"She didn't lose her job. She resigned. And anyway, that situation was entirely different."

"Why?"

"Because she was an adult and in a position of responsibility."

I sighed.

"So when all of us reach the age of eighteen we should have miraculously gained the ability not to make these verbal blunders. I'll look forward to that."

"Anyway, stop trying to change the subject. I want you to promise me that you will give Tim a chance."

"I don't see the point."

"Anna ... this really could be your chance to experience a relationship. You've wanted this to happen for so long, and now that the opportunity is in front of you, you're ignoring it."

"I simply don't believe that this is my one and only chance. And if it is, I might pass."

"I'm not suggesting that it's your one and only chance. I'm suggesting that it's a chance. The only way you're going to find love is if you ... if you accept it when it's offered."

"You honestly think that *Tim Stademan* is the best that I can do?"

"Anna, that's a horrible thing to say."

"Why is it? It's how I feel."

"Because Tim is intelligent, interesting, kind and reliable. He's also had a pretty shit life, from what I can gather. He has done nothing but put himself out for you, and this is the reaction he gets from you. Your disdain."

I felt my throat begin to tighten and my eyes turn hot. Tears started to form at the corners of my eyes.

"Look, I know I'm not exactly being fair to him, but the truth is I just don't *want* him."

"No. The truth is that you just don't want to be seen to want him."

"*What*?!"

"You want someone with a better image. So you can show the world how normal you are."

Tears started trickling down my cheeks.

"So who's being horrible now?" I asked, miserably.

"I'm *sorry*, Anna. I'm not trying to be horrible. But this is too important. I want you to search your heart and to be honest with yourself. Is it Tim that's the problem? Or what the rest of the world will think when they see you with him? And if it's the latter, you may be destined to a very lonely life. That is all I have to say."

And with that, she hung up on me. I couldn't believe it. I slid under the duvet, curled up into a tight ball and cried myself to sleep.

Chapter Twenty-Three

The wires were cut with unexpected ease.

Dr. Poole used a pair of wire-cutters that would not have looked out of place in my father's garage. With six firm snips he sliced through the wires that held my jaws and my 44 days of imprisonment came to an end.

But at the crucial moment, my jaws remained firmly together. I touched my mouth and looked anxiously at Dr. Poole.

"What's going on? Why can't I open it?"

"It'll take a while," he said. "A few days, maybe a week or two. The muscles will need to relax and to gain strength. It will come, with time. For now, you'll have to take it very slowly."

I couldn't believe it. No-one had told me this. For six weeks I had been waiting for this moment, and now yet more patience was required. I wanted to cry.

"As soon as your muscles are working, you'll need to book yourself in with Dr. Isaac for the next phase of orthodontic work," said Dr. Poole.

I stared at him in disbelief.

"*The next phase*?! What the hell are you talking about?"

Dr. Poole shifted uncomfortably in his chair.

"Well. Um. First of all you will need to see the hygienist and the dentist to clean up the backs of your teeth and to make sure that there isn't any damage. You haven't been able to clean them properly for six weeks."

"Obviously."

"Then you will need a brace to bring the teeth on the right hand side together – at the moment the top ones do not meet the bottom ones due to the altered shape of your jaw."

"I see. And how long will that take?"

"Er, I'm not sure. I'm not an expert on the orthodontic side of things. Six to eight months, maybe?"

"Great. Anything else?"

"After that, Dr. Isaac will need to design a retainer to encourage the jaws not to slip back into their old position."

"A retainer."

"Yes. Another plastic removable piece that you will have to wear all the time for one year or so, and then at night for as long as you can keep it up."

I nodded miserably.

Dr. Poole cleared his throat.

"There is also the probability that you will require more surgery. Nothing like as major as what you've just been through, but some tidying up work."

"What sort of tidying up work?"

"When I transplant flesh in this kind of procedure, I always move a little more than I think is required."

"Why? Why would you do that?"

"Because it's almost impossible to judge it absolutely right during surgery, and while we can always operate to remove a little excess, we simply can't operate to add more in. It's not cushion stuffing; you can't just keep shoving it in and plumping up the pillow until it looks right. The process is a little bit more complicated than that, Anna."

I sighed and nodded. There was no escaping the fact that I still had a long way to go. Surgery might be my closest thing to a miracle, but I ought to have learnt by now that medical miracles are a slow and painful process.

"Anyway!" said Dr. Poole. "That's all in the future. For now, focus on the fact that you need to get those jaws working. Take it gently, of course, but don't be afraid; the bones have healed well and it's time to get things moving. Apart from anything, it's obvious that you will need to regain some weight."

No-one had discussed my obvious weight loss with me up until now. Mum and I had been sent to see a dietician in the early stages of my liquid diet, but we had both agreed that she was a complete idiot and didn't bother with her after that. We didn't need a dietician to tell us that I could only drink energy shakes and that I was slowly losing weight.

"I can't wait to start eating normally," I said. "As

soon as I can cram something into my mouth, rest assured that I am going to be eating it!"

Dr. Poole nodded.

"I'm not worried," he said. "You'll soon put the weight back on and I assume you have no plans to enter the Marathon this summer."

I snorted and Dr. Poole smiled.

"Just contact the dietician if you have any questions."

"Hmmm. I am sure she'll have some terrific pearls of wisdom. Like the suggestion that I need to eat more. Brilliant. Give the woman a pay rise."

Dr. Poole waggled his finger at me.

"Don't knock the dieticians," he said. "They have a very important role in the NHS."

"Yeah. It must take a lot of training to develop your skills in stating the obvious."

I distinctly saw that Dr. Poole was hiding the trace of a smirk as he turned to put his notes into my medical file.

"See you next month, Anna. I'm looking forward to it already."

Chapter Twenty-Four

The weeks and months that followed passed with increasing haste. I continued to see Dr. Poole and Dr. Isaac on a regular basis, and slowly but surely my face took shape. The extreme irregularity that nature had given me faded away, and in its place was left a more balanced appearance.

As the weeks and months slipped by, I started to realise that strangers were treating me differently. Gone were the furtive glances from passers-by, gone was the over-compensatory cheerfulness of shopkeepers. On one momentous day in Kingston, I realised that I was being treated with the same level of disdain or mild disinterest as any other shopper. Ashley and I went for a triumphant meal in Pizza Express to celebrate my new status as an Apparently Normal Person.

Dr. Isaac continued to torment me with the promised brace and retainer, and there were still times when the process seemed unbearable. One version of the first brace I simply refused to wear. Another was painful, but achieved good results.

The retainer that followed it was manageable but frustrating, and I longed for the day when it would be only a night-time necessity.

School became more intense with every month that passed. Ashley and Harry split up, but remained good friends. Ashley and I started attending a Debating Club and Harry developed a passion for chess. Before we knew it, we were entering the 6th Form and starting our A level subjects. Ashley went ahead with Maths and the Sciences, but Miss Khan did get her wish: Ashley chose RE as her fifth subject at A level.

"They like medics with another string to their bow," she told me. "It doesn't do for us all to be nothing but number-bods."

I thought about the scores of doctors that I had encountered over the years and agreed.

Tim remained a part of my life and continued to visit as often as he could. Sometimes we returned to London together and he showed me round some more of the galleries and museums. His Mum continued to suffer with her MS but her condition was stable. She even joined us at a restaurant for lunch one Sunday, and my parents were delighted to see her out and about.

I thought often about the harsh words that Ashley had said to me about Tim, and reflected on the extent to which I agreed with them. Maybe I had judged him on his appearance, and maybe I was too worried about what the rest of the world would think of him as a potential partner. Maybe I had spent so many years suffering the curious glances of strangers that I could not bear the thought of attaching myself to someone who might attract a similar reaction.

Maybe, maybe. Who knows?

With every day that passed, life somehow seemed a little bit less like a problem to be solved. Tim's presence in my life was a simple fact that seemed to settle into its stride over time, and I was glad of it. Maybe one day I would think harder about the nature of our relationship. Right now, I wasn't ready to decide.

My studies took up much of my attention, as my ambition was to study English at University. Unlike Ashley, my talents lay in subjects like History and Drama, but favourite of all was English. By the time we were halfway through the 6th Form I had started writing poetry. Ashley said that I was going to be a famous poet and that I must dedicate my first published collection to her.

I studied many poems during my remaining years at school, but none have come back to me with the same recurring power as the one by Andrew Marvell. I think of it often, and remember how those *deserts of vast eternity* spoke to me as I waited for the huge wheels of time to grind their way forward. Mum had tried to make me see the real meaning of those deserts, but I had not been ready to hear her. Now I was just beginning to understand the sense of urgency and joy contained in that poem, and it thrilled me.

The poem finishes with the image of the sun, which I believe stands for time itself. Marvell points out that we cannot physically stop time: that's not possible. But if we make the most of the time that we have, then somehow it will seem to start flying. The only way to beat the sun is to chase it.

Thus, though we cannot make our sun stand still,
Yet we will make him run.

To read more of Anna's story you can follow her blog.

Go to www.emmacwilliams.com.

Follow the author on Twitter @emma_c_williams.